TOPLINERS

General Editor: Aidan Chambers

The Dragon in the Garden

Jimmy Stewart was thirteen before he ever went to
school. And as soon as he got there he was in trouble —
trouble with the masters and trouble with the boys. But
worst of his troubles was Fagso Brown, the tough gang
leader who terrorized the school with his 'protection
racket'. From then on, it's open war between Jimmy and
Fagso — and the things that happen include an adventure
with high explosives ... and two near-drownings. The
action's fast and furious and reaches a thrilling climax in
the final battle of the boys.

TOPLINERS

The Dragon in the Garden

Reginald Maddock

Macmillan

First published 1968
Reprinted 1968, 1971, 1972, 1973, 1974, 1976, 1977, 1978,
1979, 1980, 1981, 1982, 1983, 1985 (twice), 1986

Published by
MACMILLAN EDUCATION LTD
Houndmills, Basingstoke, Hampshire RG21 2XS
and London
Companies and representatives
throughout the world

Printed in Hong Kong

ISBN 0–333–04242–5

Contents

1 The Dragon in the Garden

I didn't go to school when I was a little kid. I'll tell you how it was.

My mother didn't believe in schools in those days and when she doesn't believe in a thing my father usually doesn't believe in it either. He's a big quiet man whose eyes smile more often than his lips and he doesn't bother much about anything except the raw red clay he fashions into pots. If you ever want to see strength and love give birth to beauty you watch my father's hands as they mould the wet clay.

My mother helps him. Most of all she helps him by designing the pots. The swift precision of her brush on paper was something I always wanted to show off to other kids. The trouble was I never knew any other kids well enough.

I didn't go to school until we came to Farley and I was just thirteen then. Before we came to Farley my mother educated me. When I was a little kid she wrote a lot of letters to some Government Minister and he gave in after a long time and agreed that she could educate me. My father said that it would have been easier for the Minister if he'd given in right at the very start because my mother always did things her own way. She educated me her own way. She taught me some of the usual old things so that they seemed to be new discoveries. Arithmetic with her wasn't about multiplication tables or how many pennies in a hundred pounds. It was about weights of clay, capacities of pots, costs of materials, percentage profits. Science was about kiln temperatures or the chemistry of glazes. English was about books. She bought books in crates and I soaked them up as a thirsty desert soaks up rain. My father helped her. He taught me the most important thing of all. He taught me how to look at things so that I saw them the way they should be seen.

If we hadn't gone to Farley my mother would have kept on educating me.

Farley's in the north Midlands, near enough to hills for them to be seen. They pile up to the west, lumpy, brooding hills that were there long before Farley, and Farley's so old that the Romans knew it. They went there to make the red clay into pots. It was the clay took my father there.

He bought Farley Farm, an old house with stone floors and beams that glow like wine. Every night that house creaks in the darkness as it stretches its old timbers. It scared me a bit at first until I got to know the house and felt the friendliness of it.

My father turned the outbuildings into drying-rooms, store-rooms and a throwing-room with two potter's wheels in it. He had a couple of big electric kilns installed in the stable, and in the wall of one of the spare bedrooms he had the builders knock a great rectangular hole which they filled with glass so that my mother had a studio.

All that was done before we moved. For a week after we moved we worked every day until bedtime. I wasn't very big but I was strong enough and I did my share. When I think now of that week I remember work and blind tiredness and meals eaten at odd times off the top of a crate. But we must have finished the work because I remember a morning when there was nothing for me to do. The spring sunshine was flooding the kitchen floor and it drew me outside.

The air was soft and warm and luminous with sunlight. We never had air like that in London. I looked at the garden. The land once farmed from the house had gone, taken over by other farms, but the big garden had been left. To me, used only to the shorn greenness and regimented trees of parks, that garden was a paradise where weeds and shrubs and brambles rioted and where birds had no need to be fed breadcrumbs and pea-nuts. My mother called it the wilderness, but a grown-up's wilderness can be a kid's paradise.

I walked into it, pushing through a clump of juvenile sycamores which would never have been left to grow with such untidy naturalness in a gardener's garden. I ploughed on through shoulder-high grass, skirting nettles and brambles, my stomach aching with an explorer's excitement. If the place had ever known a gardener there was nothing left to show that he had worked there, neither form nor shape nor any of the prim plants that gardeners cherish, until, a hundred yards from the house, I came across fruit trees, twisted old apples and pears with scabby bark, which had produced no fruit for

9

years. Beyond the trees was the end of the garden. I knew that it was the end of the garden because I found a fence-post, brown and withered like an old bone, with a tendon of rusty wire still clinging to it.

Outside the garden I was on somebody else's land. On both sides I could see a pattern of fields, but the neck of land behind our garden was untended, probably because it lifted sharply into a hill on which gorse sparkled among the grass. Right in front of me there was a quarry where at one time men had dug into the hillside for the stone used in the building of so many of the houses in Farley.

For some reason I was afraid of that quarry. I stood in front of it in the bright sunshine and I was afraid. Birds and insects were making the air sing and hum all round me yet I feared the quarry because it was filled with silence and shadows.

'You're a coward!' I said aloud, and I walked straight in, thrusting aside the grass and the twining brambles.

The walls of the quarry climbed quickly above me and, once inside, I was no longer afraid. It was silent and shadowy, but it was peaceful. It was a place I liked being in; a silent place where a boy could think secret thoughts and do secret things.

Then I came to the end of the quarry. The old rock rose straight for fifty feet and I stopped in front of it and my spine tingled right up into my neck. There was a dragon on the rock. At the bottom of the rock-face there was a little cave where quarrymen had at one time started to drive a shaft. Fairly recently a big slab of rock had fallen from above the cave and on the fresh face of new rock — rose-pink and gritty — there was a red dragon about three feet tall. It was running on two wide-striding back legs. Its spine swept round in an arc, its head was thrown up and its spiky jaws gaped in agony. All its bones were there in the rock, red and burnished, and I knew that they had been there long before the quarry was dug, before the hill became a hill. I knew that the dragon was a fossil, its bones for ever cemented in the shape of cruel death.

The blood thrilled in my veins as I reached up to touch the dragon and felt my fingers run along the steely smoothness of those old bones. It was my dragon; my secret.

Then somebody sniggered behind me and I swung round. I was flushed and panting.

There were two boys in the quarry. One of them was big and the other small and ratty, and I knew with a boy's quick understanding that they were both older than I was. They were dressed in leather jackets and faded blue jeans. It was the big boy I watched. He had shoulders so broad they bulged the leather of his jacket and over his big head a mop of long hair was hanging. His eyes seemed to be hating something.

'Who're you?' he rumbled at me. 'What're you doin' here? Scarper!'

I didn't know much about kids but I knew that this one was bad and dangerous, yet I wasn't afraid. I never was afraid of anything I could see and I could see him all right.

'I'm Jimmy Stewart,' I told him, 'and I'm here because I want to be here. Who are you?'

'Cheeky!' the smaller boy said. 'Posh, too. He wants the treatment, Fagso.'

He had a mean little face and hair so thin you knew he was going to be bald before he had been a man for many years. I was trying to understand his whining words when the big boy said, 'Cripes! Look at that!' He was staring at my dragon. 'This kid's been drawin'! You done that, kid?'

I snorted. I knew a chimpanzee in London Zoo more intelligent than these two.

'It's a fossil,' I said. 'Don't you know a fossil when you see one?'

Fagso's fingers raked among his greasy hair and the other boy sniggered.

'You know any fossils, Nicker?' Fagso asked him.

'Old Mason!' Nicker bleated. He grinned at me. 'Old Mason's the headmaster at our school, kid, and he's a right old fossil.'

'That don't look much like old Mason,' Fagso said, nodding at my dragon. 'Old Mason's uglier than that.'

He took a packet of cigarettes from his pocket and opened it, Nicker's eyes watching with an addict's concentration. Fagso drew out a cigarette, looked at it and pushed it towards Nicker who said, 'Ta! See you right, Fagso, when I've got some.'

Fagso waited until his cigarette was burning and then, blinking at me through the smoke, he said, 'Want one, kid?'

I'd never tried to smoke. Neither my father nor my mother had ever smoked in all the time I'd known them.

Fagso was watching me, his eyes despising me, and Nicker said, 'He's a kid, Fagso! It's a waste of a fag!'

I took a cigarette from the offered packet and put it clumsily into my mouth. Fagso blew the ash off the end of his cigarette and held it to mine.

'Pull, kid,' he said.

I sucked in. I felt the smoke in my mouth and I blew it out. I sucked again and the smoke was in my throat, twisting it and tearing it, and I started to cough. I coughed until the world turned red and all the time I could hear Fagso's booming laugh and Nicker's yelp.

'You're a scream, Fagso!' he gasped. 'You're a bloomin' riot! It was worth a fag to see that!'

'It was worth one of mine,' Fagso said.

Slowly I fought down the coughing and I brushed the tears from my eyes. I was still holding the cigarette, its middle flattened between my finger and thumb. I tapped and squeezed it plump while my scorched throat settled, and I sucked at it again. This time it wasn't so bad. It tasted like the fumes from a dirty chimney, but it burned my throat less fiercely and I went on sucking at it, breathing in its foulness, until I had almost finished it and I felt sick. My stomach was rising into my mouth.

Fagso and Nicker were laughing so hard they could barely speak. Nicker pointed a trembling finger at me.

'Look at 'im!' he shrieked. 'Looks like he saw a flippin' ghost!'

I rushed to the wall of the quarry and I was sick. Standing with my forehead pressed against the cool rock I panted while my empty stomach righted itself. I looked up and there was my dragon, still defying the world he had once terrorized. I turned back to the two boys. They had used up all their laughter and they were sitting in the grass, their backs against the wall of the quarry.

'Where you from, kid?' Fagso asked me. 'And what are you doin' here?'

I walked slowly across to them.

'You heard, kid!' Nicker snarled. 'You heard Fagso ask you. You tell him quick!'

These two were nothing like any boys I'd ever met. The only kids I really knew were my two cousins, and I saw them only each summer when I went to stay with my uncle who is a sculptor in Cornwall. My two cousins are girls. When I was with them we sometimes met other kids, but I never got to know them well. I didn't want to get to know them, really. They were such kids, so full of kids' talk.

Fagso wasn't a bit like them. He was no kid. Somehow I felt that he had never been a kid.

'You heard!' Nicker said again. 'You tell Fagso or I'll do you!'

I didn't think much of Nicker. He made me think of a weasel I'd seen in the zoo.

'You'll do me?' I said. 'What are you talking about?'

Fagso chuckled and Nicker said, 'Hark at him! He's a right one is this! Posh, too. I'll belt you, kid! That's what I mean.'

'I don't think you could,' I said.

He blinked to hide the doubt in his little eyes. He

watched me, weighing me up, his slight mind assessing his chances.

'Think I could do you, kid?' Fagso asked.

I thought for a moment or two. 'You might. You're big, but size isn't everything. We'd have to try.'

Nicker snorted. 'Ain't nobody at school Fagso can't belt! They're all scared of Fagso.'

'You ain't scared, are you, kid?' Fagso said. He was ten times quicker than Nicker. 'You ain't scared of me?'

I shook my head. 'Why should I be?'

He bunched a big fist and studied it. 'That's one reason. How about that, kid?'

'I've got two of those,' I said and showed him a fist, smaller than his but solid enough.

He grinned. 'You're a nut-case, kid. Where you from?'

'London,' I said. 'We've come to live at Farley Farm. My father's a potter and my mother's an artist.'

'Blimey!' Nicker said. 'My old man's a brickie's labourer and my old woman's a char.'

'You wanna watch it, kid,' Fagso said. 'Livin' in the old house, I mean. There's ghosts in it.'

'I haven't seen any,' I said.

He nodded. 'You will. You wouldn't get me in that place after dark for a fortune, and I don't get scared easy.'

'Fagso's scared of nobody,' Nicker bleated. 'He's Fagso Brown and I'm Nicker Edwards and we're mates. Everybody in Farley and Cronton and Barnton knows about us. You ask 'em. Everybody!'

' 'Specially the coppers,' Fagso said. He gave me an old, wise look. 'You wanna keep away from us, kid. We're bad and we like bein' bad. You're a nice boy and we'd make you bad. None of the mams of the nice boys let them come with us. You'd better not come here.'

'I live here.'

'Not in this quarry, you don't. This quarry doesn't belong to your old man. If anybody owns it it's old Farmer Thwaites and he never bothers with it. Nicker and me's the only ones ever come here.'

'It's ours, kid,' Nicker said. 'It's our private quarry.'

I thought of the fossil, my dragon, which I wasn't going to share with anybody.

'It isn't yours,' I said.

Nicker pointed a yellowed finger at me. 'You keep out of it, kid! And you can clear off now!'

'I'll come here any time I feel like it,' I said. 'And that'll be pretty often.'

'Beat it!' Nicker shouted. 'Go on! Beat it before I smash your face in!'

'I don't think you could,' I said.

He growled. He started to get up, but his coward's spirit failed him and he paused, crouching.

Fagso grinned and nudged him. 'You show the kid, Nicker! You ain't scared of the nice boy, are you, Nicker?'

Nicker scrambled up in front of me. I'd never had a fight in my life. I'd never seen a fight except those I sometimes saw on television. My mother had decided that I should watch some of the schools' programmes so we'd had a television set for about a couple of years. I watched other programmes, too. I could watch any programme I fancied, even the cheap sensational programmes, because my mother said they were useful in developing taste and setting standards. So I'd seen television fights and I knew there were three kinds. There was the gun-fighting of the Western, the savage, kicking fighting of the crime-film and the scientific fighting of the boxer. I knew that Nicker was neither cowboy nor gangster so I held up my hands to box him, my left fist forward and my chin on my chest.

Nicker's hands were like talons as he pranced round me, his little eyes watching me.

Fagso spat. 'Get on with it! Stop messing about! You've got to catch Nicker, kid, 'fore you can clout him. Takes a bit o' catching does Nicker.'

I glanced at Fagso, still leaning back against the rock, and in a second Nicker rushed in, grabbed my hair and jerked my face down on to his hard skull. I smelled the sweat and grease of his scalp, but then I smelled nothing. My nose was crushed and bleeding and tears were blinding my eyes.

Fagso gave a bellow. 'You're learnin', Nicker!'

I clutched my face in both hands and while I was lost and blinded something hit me hard in the stomach and doubled me up. I heard Nicker's triumphant squeal.

'How's that, Fagso?' he yelled.

'You're gettin' good, Nicker,' Fagso growled. 'You best come and have another fag 'fore you do yourself an injury.'

I was huddled on the ground. My nose was still bleeding, but I could breathe again and my eyes were clearing. I don't know if I wept, but I think my only tears were tears of pain. I was thinking. I was thinking that I had tried the wrong kind of fighting. Nicker used the tricks of the gangster, but I could use them too.

I glanced up. Fagso had his cigarettes out again and Nicker was strutting about like a champion, shadow-boxing, punching the air and snorting.

'Sit down!' Fagso said. 'Beltin' the kid'll be goin' to your head. You'll be tryin' me next.'

'Not you, Fagso!' Nicker said. He punched again. 'You're me mate. But the kid! I smashed him up!'

He didn't see me coming. I was on my feet and behind him in a second. While he glowed and exulted I grabbed his greasy hair, spun him round and sent my knee crashing into his stomach. He gasped and slumped forward and my hand chopped down like an axe on to the back of his neck. He didn't make a sound. He went on his face into the grass and I kicked him in the ribs.

'Hey!' Fagso shouted, jumping to his feet and dropping his cigarette.

I drew my foot back for another kick, but my shoulder was suddenly gripped and I was flung aside. I saw Fagso charge away towards the old fruit trees, and my father bend over Nicker and turn him on to his back.

My father is a very big man. He turned Nicker easily and Nicker groaned and opened his eyes and his eyes stayed open, staring. He saw my huge father crouching over him: he saw a man with wild hair and clay daubs on his face. Terror impelled

Nicker to his feet and he ran.

My father smiled and said, 'Not much wrong with that youth.'

He put his hand on my shoulder and he led me slowly back towards the house and he talked in that way of his, so that you never know whether he's talking to you or to himself.

'He's a dirty little rat,' he said. 'But you floored him and kicked him when he was down and that was wrong. You turned yourself into a dirty little rat to beat him. You can only learn to live with others by living with others. I should have seen this coming. A boy needs to go to school.'

2 School

So it was arranged for me to go to school and that Government Minister chap in London must have smiled when he heard about it. The school I had to go to was Cronton Comprehensive which is about a couple of miles from Farley. I started as soon as the Easter holidays were over.

My mother didn't argue. She makes most of the decisions, but once in a while my father decides something and my mother never argues. It was like that when he decided to move from London to Farley. She must have preferred London where there are galleries and concerts and other artists, but my father preferred Farley where there's clay. She didn't argue. Something in his eyes or his voice it is that gives him a sort of authority which can't be argued against. That was how it was when he told her that I was going to school. She didn't argue. That same day she got our little car out of the barn and drove to Cronton and when she came back it was all fixed up. She'd even bought me the uniform, a grey blazer with a badge on the pocket and a green tie.

Cronton Comprehensive's a boys' school. There's one at Farley for girls. The kids go to them when they're eleven and leave when they're fourteen to go to Barnton Senior Comprehensive.

I'd never seen Cronton School until the morning I started there. My mother took me in the car, dropping me at the gate.

She grinned at me and said, 'Now it's up to you.'

I walked straight in, looking forward in an odd, excited way to being the same as other kids. The school was just as my mother had described it, a grouping of shoe-box shapes made of concrete and glass, with the brilliant green of an overgrown playing-field stretching away behind it towards the distance where the hills were.

I walked along the front of the school and round a corner and I was in the playground. In front of me were hundreds of boys doing the things I had never done. They were wrestling and rolling and screaming and shouting. They were darting and dashing so swiftly that the patterns of their movements made me dizzy, while their noise deafened me.

In a corner of the playground I met loneliness for the first time in my life. Loneliness isn't being alone but wondering why you have to be alone. I had rarely known other kids, I had always been alone, yet in those first moments at school I felt loneliness flood through me as I watched the hundreds of boys. My brain ached as their uproar beat against it. They and I were all wearing the same uniform, but they were different from me. They were rough savages, screaming their war-cries and rushing into brutal battle, and they were happy in a way I had never known. They were happy shouting at each other, wrestling each other, hating each other.

Then one of them spotted me and, like a dog catching a strange scent, he swerved and stopped in front of me. He was smaller than I was and younger and his thick glasses gave him the look of an owl.

'You a new kid?' he asked.

I nodded.

'What's your name?'

'Stewart,' I said. He was shooting his questions at me like bullets and I didn't like them.

'Stewart what?' he asked.

'Jimmy Stewart.'

'Jimmy Stewart,' he said as if tasting the name. Then he went into a convulsive dance and started screaming, '*Jimmy Stewpot! Jimmy Stewpot!*'

I was so astonished that I just stared at him and didn't at first see the other boys his voice had attracted. They came gathering round and while he went on jerking like a Dervish they studied me. He was red-faced and hoarse, his spectacles were on the end of his nose, he was a nightmare of a boy yet they watched me.

'He's a new kid!' he yelled. 'His name's Jimmy Stewpot!'

I could see dozens of pairs of eyes and I knew how zoo animals must feel on Sunday afternoons when people press close to the cages. There was a dull kind of interest in all the eyes; interest and animosity, but no friendliness. I felt lonelier than ever.

Suddenly the crowding boys were torn apart and a boy I had seen before was there. It was Fagso, in a tatty uniform, looking like a man impersonating a schoolboy.

'It's the killer,' he said, grinning at me. 'Fancy that! The killer's come to school!'

'You seen him before, Fagso?' the spectacled boy asked.

Fagso nodded. 'You wanna keep away from him, Specky. All the little First-Year kids wanna keep away from him. He's the one smashed up Nicker the other day.'

They stared at me with fresh interest and some curiosity.

Specky yelled, 'He's Stewpot! I'm not scared of Stewpot!'

'You'd be petrified if you saw him fightin',' Fagso said. 'He fights dirty. He kicks kids when they're down. Don't you, Stewpot?'

He pointed a thick finger at me. 'You'd best watch it, kid. There's some ain't going to like what you did to Nicker. Nicker's got friends and they're liable to beat you up. How would it be if I stuck up for you? If I tell 'em to lay off they'll lay off.'

' 'S'right,' Specky said. 'If you pay Fagso a bob a week he looks after you and nobody clouts you. I've brought my bob for this week, Fagso.'

'Playtime,' Fagso said. 'You give it Nicker at playtime and he'll tick your name in the book and you'll be O.K. for the week. Won't be anybody'll dare to lay one on you if you're one of my kids. You other kids, too. You pay your bobs to Nicker.' He gave me a prod in the chest. 'How about it, kid? You want protection? You want to be one of my boys?'

'I'll look after myself,' I said.

Fagso sighed. 'We've got a right one 'ere! I'm going to have him seen to.'

Scores of boys were now pressing round, jeering at me, despising me, thinking me a lunatic.

'Do him, Fagso!' Specky urged, anxious for a sacrifice. 'Go on, do him!'

Some of the others took it up. 'Smash him, Fagso! Beat him up!'

Fagso shook his head. 'No need. There's others'll do it. He's a bit little for me. If I hit him I'd kill him, likely enough.' He grinned at me. 'When Nicker sees you, kid, he'll throw a fit. He'll go mad. Nobody'll be able to hold him back. Except me, and I won't 'cos you haven't paid your bob.'

Somewhere a whistle shrilled thinly and the boys scattered and left me in the corner with Fagso. He spat. Then lazily he gave me a slap on the side of the head that made my ear smart and hum.

'You know what's good for you, kid,' he said, 'and you'll pay your bob. You'll be one of Fagso's boys.'

He turned and slouched away and I saw a brown, tweedy man with a whistle clamped between his teeth and I knew that he must be one of the masters. I went to him.

Without taking the whistle out of his mouth he said, 'Who are you?'

I couldn't speak. I had forgotten who I was. At that moment I was a lonely tragic boy who could remember nothing of what he had been.

'Are you a new boy?' he asked me, and I nodded.

He gave another blast on the whistle. 'You'd better go to the Head. Through that door.' He pointed. 'Go along the corridor and you'll find the office at the far end. Knock.'

I was in a new world. I went through strange alien rites. I met the Headmaster and an oldish woman who lived in the lavender-scented atmosphere of an office next to the Head's. They asked me questions and wrote in books and, when it was over, the lavender secretary took me through the school, chattering to me endlessly and only stopping when we met a master, a small bustling man with a black gown and a bristly moustache.

'Mr. Harris!' she sang.

He scowled and said nothing.

'A new boy for you, Mr. Harris,' she said. 'James Stewart. Mr. Mason says he'll have a word with you later.'

Mr. Harris didn't even look at me. He said, 'Wait in my room, boy,' and walked away.

The lavender secretary whispered, 'It's the room at the end,' and went clicking along the corridor in pursuit of him.

I found the room at the end of the corridor. Its door was open and there was an excited noise inside it. As soon as I went in the noise stopped, switched off. The boys stared at me, and a paper aeroplane, floating in the air, slid unheeded to the floor.

'It's that new kid,' somebody said. 'Old Mason's put him in 2E.'

'Charlie isn't going to like that,' somebody else said. 'It'll give him more marking than ever.'

There must have been thirty boys sitting mostly in pairs at desks. I'd never seen so many boys in one tight group. I stood out there at the front, exposed and solitary, and I saw them as thirty segments of one body.

'They call him "Stewpot",' one of them said. 'Specky Miller out of 1R christened him.'

There was a titter.

'Fagso Brown's going to have him seen to,' another of them said, and there was a groan.

Near to me, at the front of the class, was a red-haired boy with eyes as blue as innocence.

'You better watch out for Fagso, kid,' he said. 'Fagso's tough. He's tougher than any kid in school. You're O.K. if you're one of his boys, but you watch out if you aren't.'

The boy next to him slowly poked his inkwell with a pencil. He nodded. He was bigger than the other boys in the room and his hair was so close-cropped that his scalp shone through it.

'There's three you've got to watch out for,' he said. 'Fagso, old Mason and Charlie Harris.'

'Charlie's the worst of the teachers!' somebody called from the back of the room and there was an instant's uneasy silence while they all listened for footsteps in the corridor.

'Charlie's dead easy if you know how,' the red-haired boy said. 'How about if we tell the new kid? How about if we help him a bit? Then he won't have to suffer like we did.'

One or two of the boys wriggled and grinned and somebody said, 'You tell him, Ginger! Go on!'

The big boy said, 'You'll be O.K., Evans. Fagso'll look after you.'

Ginger's smile and voice were smooth. 'It's like this, kid. Charlie Harris is our Form Master. You

26

seen him yet? A little chap with a 'tache and a face like sudden death?'

I nodded. 'I saw him in the corridor.'

'Posh!' Ginger said. 'Talks like that chap on the telly, this kid!'

'Get on with it!' the big boy growled at him. 'You were on about Charlie Harris. It was your idea.'

'You saw Charlie, kid,' Ginger said. 'You saw him when he was going to see old Mason about dinner-money. Dinner-money drives Charlie bonkers. He can never get it right. You've got to bring it the first day of every week and you haven't got to want any change. You brought yours?'

I pulled a handful of silver out of my pocket. 'My mother said it would be five shillings.'

Ginger beamed. 'You've got a clever mother, Stew. You give Charlie five bob and you'll be over the first danger. The other one's this. You don't ever call him "Charlie". Not to his face I mean. You call him "Charlie" and he'll bury you. You've got to call him "Charles". What school were you at last?'

'I've never been to school before,' I said.

They gaped at me and somebody said, 'Can you read?'

'Of course I can,' I said. 'My mother and father have been educating me.'

There was a snigger. A little boy on the front row said, 'I'd like to see my dad educating me! He can't do my homework sums now!'

Ginger Evans winked at somebody and then looked again at me, his voice all friendliness, his eyes brilliant with mischief.

'Thought you might have been used to calling

teachers "sir",' he said. 'You don't do that with Charlie. He's one of these modern teachers. You call him "Charles" and you stick "Charles" on to everything you say if you don't want him to belt you. "Yes, Charles." That's how you do it. "Thanks very much, Charles." Got it? You do that and you'll be O.K. That right, you lot?'

They were nodding and grinning, and one or two of them were near to bursting.

'You must think everybody's as daft as you are, Evans,' the big boy said.

Ginger didn't hear him. He was too anxious to fill me with information. 'Charlie's got a stick, kid. Keeps it in that cupboard. Most of the teachers don't cane you but Charlie does and Timber Thompson sometimes. Gutsy Collins — he takes P.T. — he uses a slipper. But Charlie's the one to watch. If he uses his stick on you it feels like you've been guillotined. So you give him five bob for your dinners so's he can spend it on whisky at night and you call him "Charles" and you'll be O.K. That's how we do it. Isn't that right, you lot?'

There were frenzied nods and giggles which were strangled when Mr. Harris walked into the room. He looked at me.

'You're the new boy. Stewart, is it?'

'Yes, Charles,' I said.

There was a network of tiny purple veins over his cheeks and these were suddenly lost in the redness that flushed into his face. His bottom lip was slightly trembling.

'Somebody told you to say that,' he said and the trembling of his lip became a trembling of his voice.

'Somebody told you to address me in that way. Who was it, Stewart?'

I nodded at Ginger. 'This boy told me your name.'

'When you address me, Stewart,' Mr. Harris said, 'call me "sir". "Sir", boy.' He went to the cupboard beside the blackboard and without looking at the class he said, 'Come out, Evans!'

Ginger came out, his face brighter than his hair. As he walked past me he punched me in the stomach so hard that I gasped.

'*Snitch!*' I heard somebody whisper.

The boys were glaring at me; all except the big boy next to Ginger. He was smiling a little as he watched me, a shy embarrassed smile.

Mr. Harris was holding his cane. It was about three feet long and half an inch thick and it had the cruel curve of a scimitar.

'Your hand, Evans,' he said. 'This is for impertinence.'

Ginger's jaw was set tight and his mouth was a thin straight line. Mr. Harris raised the cane and held it high for an immeasurable time while he watched Ginger's unwilling hand like a cat watching a mouse. Then the cane came cutting down across the hand and Ginger jerked and lifted up his right foot.

'The other hand, Evans,' Mr. Harris said. His red face had gone pale and it was damp and shiny. 'This is for trying to get somebody else into trouble.'

Slowly Ginger offered his left hand and I watched the horrifying execution a second time and saw Ginger with his arms across his chest and his hands squeezed under his armpits go back to his desk and hate me with his eyes. I felt that I had shrunk.

'Now you, Stewart,' Mr. Harris said. 'You knew that you were being impertinent so I shall give you one stroke. Hold out your hand.'

I stared at the monster. He was the first teacher I had ever known and he tortured boys into submission. He was something out of a horror-comic and I was not afraid of him.

'No!' I said.

There was a breath from the boys and I felt their sympathy suddenly encourage me. Mr. Harris, puzzled and uncertain, blinked at me. He was having a new experience and its strangeness baffled him.

'I told you to hold out your hand,' was all he could say.

'No, Mr. Harris,' I said.

'You refuse my punishment, Stewart?'

'I haven't done anything, Mr. Harris.'

The boys were as silent as death and yet I knew that they were cheering me. Not one of them dared make a sound which might turn Mr. Harris on to him yet all of them were willing me to further defiance. I felt a kind of glory I had never known before.

'Get out!' Mr. Harris whispered at me. 'Wait in the corridor!'

I heard the Form give a sigh as I closed the door behind me and then I was in the corridor with its polished floor and rain-grimed windows where already, on this first day of term, boy artists had fingered faces and names.

Then Mr. Harris came sweeping past me and, tossing 'Come with me!' over his shoulder, went marching down the corridor. I followed him.

When we reached the office he went inside and left me to stand and listen to the distant tuneless singing of a group of boys, the thump of mallets on chisels and the droning voice of a master teaching something he'd been teaching for years — school sounds which were new to me.

The door opened and the secretary beckoned to me with one imperious finger. I followed her lavender scent to the Headmaster's room and I walked in. Behind me the door was closed with a soft hiss of air, like the door of a tomb, and I was standing in front of the Headmaster again.

He was sitting at his desk. He was a tall man with a thin and thoughtful face and his suit seemed to have been made for a fatter man. Mr. Harris was standing beside the desk. His wrath and my unrepentance made an embarrassing mixture for the Headmaster. He cleared his throat.

'You've very soon distinguished yourself, Stewart,' he said.

I didn't understand that so I said nothing.

He waited for a moment and then went on, 'You've been impertinent to Mr. Harris.'

I'd been impertinent to nobody, but some instinct told me that boys don't argue with headmasters so I still said nothing.

He tried again. 'Do you know what "impertinent" means?'

I nodded. 'But I didn't know it was impertinent.'

'I suppose there's some truth in that,' he said,

thinking, 'but ignorance is no excuse, Stewart. You also refused to be punished by Mr. Harris.'

'I hadn't done anything to be punished for.'

'You'd been impertinent.' The Headmaster stared at me. 'You agree that to address a master by his first name is an impertinence?'

'I suppose so if it's a sort of rule of the school. But I didn't know. One of the boys told me that I had to do that.'

'But it was impertinent?'

I wondered how many more times I needed to admit it. 'I said it was.'

He nodded. 'Then you should be punished. Yet you refused punishment and Mr. Harris has brought you to me. I am supposed to punish you.' He stared thoughtfully at the top of his desk and went on, 'Why did you refuse to be punished, Stewart?'

'Because I hadn't done anything.'

'But you'd been impertinent.'

'I didn't know it was impertinent, did I?' I wasn't afraid of these two men but I was growing angry. 'And it wasn't only that. It was the cane. I'm not being caned by anybody.'

The Head's reasonable voice went on while Mr. Harris breathed in so hard I thought he must burst.

'Boys are sometimes caned, Stewart. Occasionally I cane a boy. If I think it is necessary to cane you I shall cane you. Understand that, while you're in this school, I take the place of your parents.'

'My parents don't cane me,' I said hotly. 'My mother calls it beastly and barbaric. If my parents don't cane me nobody else should.'

They were both staring at me. Then Mr. Harris swung away and made for the door, but the Headmaster's quiet voice stopped him. The Headmaster stood up slowly and his height surprised me. He was taller even than my father yet he had only half my father's breadth. His eyes were blue and wise and, at that moment, twinkling. I had the sudden thought that if he caned a boy the boy deserved it.

He said, 'I don't want any boy's first day at this school to be unhappy, Stewart. A school should be a happy place because it's full of people working and playing together. I'll put your behaviour down to ignorance. You put it down to experience. Now wait in the corridor and then Mr. Harris will take you back to his room.'

I don't know what they said while I waited outside. I never did understand what gives grown-ups the right to talk about kids and keep them waiting outside closed doors while they do it. I know I was about ten minutes in that corridor before Mr. Harris came out and walked at such speed that I had to run to keep up with him.

In the classroom the boys were waiting for us and they stared at me, their eyes examining me for signs of the Headmaster's wrath.

'Evans!' Mr. Harris said. 'Move your books to the empty desk at the back of the room. You sit there, Stewart; next to Belshaw. I want to have you not too far away from me.'

I could feel the threat in his voice. Ginger Evans was sulking. He lifted his books in two hands out of his desk and left the litter and fluff for me to clear away.

'Sit down, Stewart,' Mr. Harris said. 'You're in 2E
— my form. I shall teach you English and, possibly,
good manners and obedience, although they aren't
on the timetable.'

He went to the cupboard and Belshaw, the big
boy, gave me a shy grin.

'You watch out for Ginger,' he whispered.
'Ginger's one of Fagso's boys.'

I shrugged. Already I had to watch out for too
many people.

3 Truant

I don't recall everything that happened that first day at Cronton. I seemed to swim through a sea of strangeness in which one or two events, like rocks, broke the surface and were remembered.

There was the French Master, Mr. Dillon, who gave me a hundred lines for forgetting my books. Half the Form, all talking at the same time, spent five minutes making him understand that I was a new boy who had never had any books. Then he started jabbering at me in French and quickly found that my French was better than his because my mother had lived for years in Paris and she slipped into French as easily as I fell asleep. When I told Mr. Dillon that, although I spoke French well enough, I'd never written it or read it he shook his head in wonder and left me alone.

Then there was dinner in the dining-hall. I sat at a table with seven boys who ate like famine victims, turning forks into shovels. I was at Joe Belshaw's table and he told me about Ginger Evans.

'He's cunning is Ginger,' he said. 'He'll get you for what you did to him. You snitched, mate. That's what you did. You told Charlie Harris about him.'

'What was wrong with that?'

'Kids don't like snitches. That's what. 'Cos of you Ginger got two of the best from Charlie.'

'It was his own fault,' I said. 'He was caned because he told me to call him "Charles". Mr. Harris, I mean. He shouldn't have told me to do it if it was wrong.'

Joe gave that shy grin. 'All the same, you watch out for him. Like I told you, he's one of Fagso's boys. He pays his bob every week. You got him shifted out of his desk, as well. He didn't like that. I didn't mind. Matter of fact I was glad. I don't like Ginger. I hate him. He's always getting other kids in trouble. He got me in trouble just before Easter and Charlie sticked me. He said I'd poured ink on the floor and all the time it was him.'

'What did you do? To Ginger Evans, I mean.'

'Me?' Joe shook his head. 'I wanted to smash his face in, but I didn't. You don't lay one on any of Fagso's boys at Cronton. That way you get beaten up. When you're going home at night they wait for you. You know that wood in Holt Lane?'

I shook my head.

'You must have come along it to school,' Joe said. 'It goes down to Barnton Road where the buses wait for us. About half-way down Holt Lane there's a wood. That's where Fagso and his boys wait for you. They drag you in there and they beat you up. Fagso Brown, Nicker Edwards and two or three more. I hate all of them.'

'Then why do you stand for it?' I asked.

Joe filled his mouth again and a boy across the table jeered at me. I knew him already. He was Joss

Hardy, a sneering boy with bright eyes who didn't believe in anything.

'What would you do?' he said. 'You may have got round old Mason this morning, but nobody gets round Fagso, kid. Even the Prefects and the other Third Years keep clear of Fagso. So what could a big-head like you do?'

'I'd report him. I'd tell the Headmaster.'

Joss snorted and another boy said, 'Don't think old Mason's as soft as he was this morning. He must have been feeling happy this morning, but that doesn't happen very often. Usually he's a ruddy terror, 'specially on Fridays. You go snitching to him and he'll do you, and that won't be anything to what you'll get from Fagso afterwards. Fagso'll make you so's your own mother won't know you.'

'He's right,' Joe said. 'You don't snitch on Fagso. If he ever beats you up you don't tell anybody.'

'But you can fight him, can't you?' I said.

They all stopped eating. One boy's mouth, filled with mashed potato, stayed open while he stared wide-eyed at me. They were all staring at me. They couldn't believe that anybody could be so stupid.

'*Fight Fagso!*' somebody whispered.

Joe put a hand on my shoulder. 'You listen to me, kid,' he said, and his voice was soft and sad. 'You did all right this morning with old Charlie. You did what nobody else in 2E ever did. That right, you lot?'

They nodded and grunted. I had known since playtime that defying Mr. Harris and his cane had made me something of a hero as well as something

37

of an upstart. They admired my defiance, but they resented the new boy who had defied.

'He did all right,' Joss Hardy said, 'but he's a big-head. We don't want big-heads.'

'You shut your mouth, Hardy,' Joe said quietly. Then, to me, 'It doesn't say 'cos you did all right with Charlie that you can manage Fagso. You keep clear of Fagso. He's *murder*, I'm tellin' you. He comes from a bad home, my dad reckons. Right rough lot they are, the Browns. Fagso fights dirty. I'm the best scrapper in 2E, but Fagso'd kill me. He'd kill me with one hand in his pocket. You keep clear of him.'

Joe went back to his dinner and I to mine. Some-body started grumbling that the second course was semolina.

I remember four o'clock and going home. I remember that best of all. It was the first time I'd ever gone home from school and I wasn't ready for the rush. An escaping avalanche of boys poured out of Cronton Comprehensive, the noisy First-Year lads scampering in the lead, the more sedate Third-Year lads stalking out with conscious dignity. In five minutes the school was empty except for the deten-tion room and a noise in the library, and the aproned cleaning-women had emerged and were sweeping with swift determination. The caretaker was now king.

I walked slowly through the gate and turned into the lane. I knew that down at the bottom, where the lane joined the road, the buses would be waiting. The air was full of the smell of the dust raised by hundreds of feet. I could see boys thronging the lane lower down, but I didn't try to catch them. I didn't know them.

I walked slowly, my head dizzy with newness; new faces, new buildings, new voices, new manners, a new discipline. I didn't like school and I felt sure that nobody else liked it any more than I did. The masters were sour-faced and unfriendly and the boys were only four-o'clock happy. The one thing I'd learnt all day was that school was a large number of people doing what they had to do and hating it.

I walked out of the sunlight into a black shadow across the road. I was in the shadow of the wood and on the edge of the wood was Fagso Brown, leaning against a tree and cleaning his nails with a big knife. He didn't look at me.

He said, 'You come 'ere, kid!'

'Where?' I asked.

He jerked his head. 'In here.'

'Why?'

He looked up slowly. ' 'Cos I say so.'

'I don't want to go in there,' I said. 'I'm going to the bus.'

I started to walk again and in front of me boys rushed out of the wood; Nicker Edwards, Ginger Evans and three leering boys I didn't know making a wall across the road.

'Better do like I say, kid!' Fagso called.

I kept on walking until I was stopped by the line of boys. In front of me, chest to chest, was Nicker Edwards.

'You 'eard Fagso, kid,' he said.

I was getting angry. 'Move out of my way!' I said.

39

He grinned at me. 'Think you can shift me?'

I swung a punch at his grinning face, but before my fist was half-way there he pushed me on the chest and I fell backwards over the cunning foot of one of the other boys. I sprawled on my back in the road and all five boys rushed at me. I saw Ginger Evans's snarling face dropping towards me and I swung my arm sideways and knocked it away.

Then somebody's foot ground into my stomach and squeezed the breath out of me and I was punched and kicked and picked up by the arms and legs and dropped back on to the road. My tie was pulled until I was choking and then I heard Fagso say, 'That'll do!'

The snarling, growling and grunting stopped and I lay on the road, a wreck of a boy. Slowly I got to my knees and then, scratched and torn, I stood up on wobbly legs. Fagso was in front of me.

'You snitched, kid,' he said. 'Ginger here, he got the stick from old 'arris, through you. Nobody snitches on Fagso's boys. You remember. You snitch about this and I'll do you myself tomorrow. If I do you you'll be a hospital case.'

I spat blood off my lip. My head was clearer now and I could feel the smart and ache of scratch and bruise, but stronger than these I could feel the pain of anger.

'There are six of you!' I said.

'Five, kid,' Fagso said. 'I didn't do nothin'. I just watched. Next time I'll do you myself.'

'Six!' I fumed. 'Six cowardly louts! I'll take you on now, one at a time, but you daren't! You can only fight in a pack. You're like a pack of wolves!'

'Shut your mouth, big-head!' Ginger said. 'If you don't I'll belt you!'

'You couldn't belt our Gladys!' somebody called. 'And she's only ten.'

I turned round. A crowd of boys had come from nowhere to watch the fight and in front of them was Joe Belshaw, his eyes ashamed and angry.

'You shut your mouth, Belshaw!' Ginger shouted.

'You try shuttin' it, Evans,' Joe said. 'You're pretty good fighting new kids if you've got a lot of help.'

Fagso turned his eyes on him. 'You want me to work your face over, Belshaw?'

I could see Joe fuming, but he said nothing.

'Now beat it, the lot of you!' Fagso said. 'And if anybody does any snitchin' he'll wish he hadn't.'

I picked up my books from the road and packed them under my arm and Fagso spat and said, 'A bob a week, kid, and you'll be O.K.'

'We don't want him!' Nicker said. 'He's too posh.'

'He's a big-head,' Ginger said, 'and we don't want any big-heads.'

'He pays his bob and he's O.K.' Fagso said. 'I'll do anybody that lays a finger on him. You hear, kid?'

I didn't answer him. I walked with Joe down the road, the other boys stringing out behind us. They were silent and ashamed and they were puzzled by my tearless defiance. They couldn't know that the whole way down to the bus I said nothing because I was afraid to speak. I walked firmly enough, although I was aching and burning and there was such a trembling inside me that for a time I was almost sick.

Joe said once, 'Bullies, that's what they are! Wish somebody could belt Fagso!' I heard his teeth grind together. 'If somebody smashed Fagso's face in it'd do him good. He's been in court a couple of times. Everybody says he's bad.'

The bus took me home and I walked straight into the house, into the empty kitchen, and I sat down and wept. I was still weeping when my mother came down from the studio.

'What have they been doing to my boy?' she asked in the baby voice she still sometimes used. I hated it.

I shook my head hard. 'I'm all right!'

She said, 'Tell Fiona about it.'

My father came in, looking for food, his hands red with clay. He said, 'Been playing rugger, have you, son?'

My mother frowned at him. 'He hasn't been *playing* anything, John. Can't you see?'

He looked at me closely. 'Want to tell us, Jimmy?'

I shook my head. I wasn't crying any more and my bruises weren't aching so badly but I was still trembling. Even though I concentrated all my mind on it I couldn't stop the trembling of my flesh.

'It's all right,' I said. 'Some of the boys at that school are savage. I never knew people so savage. I didn't know boys were like that.'

'They're boys,' my father said.

I said, 'They're bullies and cowards! That's what they are! I'm not going to that school any more!'

42

My voice was rising, getting higher and shriller, and my father said, 'That's all right, son.'

His quietness quietened me. 'You mean I don't have to go?'

'If you feel so strongly about it. I'm surprised that you let a few bullies and cowards stop you. Unless there's something more.'

'It's the whole school,' I said. 'Nobody's interested in you really. The teachers aren't interested. I've been there all day and I haven't learnt a thing. So I'm not going again.'

'I never thought it was a very good idea,' my mother said.

My father sat down. 'Let's have a cup of tea, Fiona; a cup of tea and some of those chocolate biscuits.'

We sat round the heavy deal table and I sipped hot tea and felt it scald my crushed lips. My mother talked about boys and bullies as if they were the same thing; about how brutes make others brutish. My father watched me and let her talk.

When I'd finished my tea he said, 'How many are there, Jimmy?'

'Bullies? Hundreds, I suppose. I met five on the way home. They were waiting for me.' I looked at the tear in my slacks, at the dusty grazes on my hands and I felt the soreness which was my ribs. 'You don't know what they did to me.'

'We don't even know what you did to them.'

'Not much. I hit one across the face, but that's all I had chance to do. There's a great big boy. He's the one who was at the quarry the other day and he looks like somebody in a crime film. He's the leader.

He was there, but he didn't do anything. He just watched.'

'The Headmaster must be told,' my mother said.

'You tell him and Fagso Brown — that's the big boy, the boss bully — he'll call it snitching and he'll beat me up, as they call it. He's got a gang, a crowd of boys he protects. They pay him a shilling a week and he looks after them and everybody's so frightened of him that nobody dares touch any of his boys.'

'You can have an extra shilling,' my father said.

I snorted. 'I'm not paying him a shilling! I'll look after myself! Anyway, I'm not going any more.'

'I knew this would happen,' my mother said.

'It had to happen some time,' my father said. 'Life isn't all art and poetry and music. There's more to it than culture. There's crudity and cruelty. There's selfishness and greed. A boy has to be exposed to all of them before he can become a man. Until he's met these things he's no defence against them. I explained all this, Fiona.'

'I know, and I wasn't convinced.'

'It happens to be true. A boy has to be in contact with the seamy side if he's ever going to get the complete picture. He doesn't understand kindness until he's known cruelty: he only recognizes nobility when he's seen meanness.' My father grinned and leaned back loosely in his chair. 'I'm being pompous, Fiona. Don't know how you put up with it. It's the only way I can explain why Jimmy should go to school. What they teach doesn't matter. What does matter is that he'll learn about living. That's what education's about. Living.'

44

'Where do I come into it?' I asked.

My father pulled his ear. 'How do you mean, son?'

'You're talking about me as if I weren't here. I'm the one who has to go to the school. What if I don't want to go?'

He stood up. 'I think you do want to go, Jimmy. I want you to go. Fiona, too. She'll want you to go.'

I looked at her. 'Do you, Fiona?'

I had always used their first names. They were the first names I had known and the first words I had spoken.

'Do you, Fiona?' I asked her again.

She shook her head and said, 'Perhaps,' and I knew that my father and I had split her loyalty between us. We sometimes did.

'She will,' he said, 'when her maternal indignation's gone off the boil.' He dug his finger into my ribs where they were sore. 'Like to help me load a kiln?'

But I didn't go to school next day. I think that was the first time I ever cheated my mother and father and I felt bad about it for months afterwards. I let them think I was going to school, because they wanted me to go, and I went out early to catch the bus, but instead I cut back through the garden to the quarry.

It wasn't that I was scared of going to school. I was always lucky that way. I didn't easily get scared and I wasn't scared of Fagso Brown and his boys or of the stone-faced teachers. I didn't go to school because I felt outraged and angry: because I thought the school wasn't a fit place to go to and wouldn't be until somebody drove the nastiness out of it and let decency in.

The quarry was a better place to be. There was neither nastiness nor savagery in the quarry. There was my dragon, but his was such an ancient savagery that it had grown beautiful. I stood in the soft sunlight and I looked at him. I knew from my books that he was a dinosaur and there could have been no beauty in his life or death. He must have been the small swift terror of his day, living in hatred. His snapping jaws and needle teeth must have invented panic. His death had been as cruel as his life. Caught by the mud he had thrown back his head to scream reptilian fury until he died in his ancient swamp. Since his death the mud had settled into rock and his bones had become a pattern of beauty. I looked at him and I thought that if his cruelty could be softened, then all cruelty could be softened.

Underneath the dragon, at the very bottom of the rock-face, there was the opening of the shaft started by the old quarrymen. I bent down to peer into it and saw that it was dark and damp; a place for creeping things and not for me.

I spent all the morning in the quarry, and the time, stolen from school, sped along at first while I explored the rock and the bushes and brambles and willowherb that turned the quarry into a jungle. Later, when there was nothing left to explore, my watch seemed to slow down, and time almost stopped.

By mid-day not even my dragon could interest me. I was hungry. The house was so near that

46

several times I heard my mother's voice and at lunchtime I heard my father whistling as he cleaned the clay from his hands. I wondered what they were eating. I could have walked through the garden and into the kitchen and my mother would have given me food and not much would have been said, yet I stayed in the quarry. It wasn't that I was afraid to go home. Instead I was ashamed. I had never cheated my mother and father before.

So I stayed in the quarry and in the early afternoon, when clouds blotted out the sun and the rain came shuttling down, I still stayed there, miserable and angry. I crept into the little cave, preferring its darkness to the wetness outside. The cave bored deeper into the rock than I had thought. What I had taken for its end was instead the beginning of blackness. I crouched in the mouth of the cave, out of the rain but uncomfortably squeezed under the low roof. The cave was no more than four feet high and above my head was all the weight of the hill. Already seeping water was beginning to drip down.

For a time I watched the rain slicing through the twigs and leaves outside. Then I turned to look into the cave. Gradually my eyes burrowed deeper as the blackness became less black and after some time I made out a shape, a geometric pattern of straight lines against the rough curves of the rock.

I spent some moments imagining and then I slowly turned myself round and crawled deeper into the cave. My body shut out the light I needed, but I reached forward and touched the sharp corner of a box. My fingers explored it. It was a wooden box about a foot and a half long and a foot wide and deep. Its corners were sheathed in metal, sandpaper-rough with rust, and it was heavy.

I drew my feet forward until I could squat over the box. I was hot and the cavern airless and the silence so great that I seemed to hear the heart of the old hill beating. I lifted the lid of the box. The hinges groaned, but the box opened easily enough and my excited fingers sank into its black inside. All they found were four bars, round and wrapped in paper, which felt like candles and were little heavier. The paper had a smooth and greasy touch. Near to the bars was a coil of thick wire covered with rough insulation.

Then I heard somebody call. Painfully I struggled round, hitting my head once on the roof, and I was almost blinded by the brilliance of the light outside. The sun was shining again and somebody was out there in the quarry.

I crawled forward, blinking and panting, and peeped out of the darkness. My father was standing only a few feet away. He was looking up at my dragon.

Without even glancing at me he said, 'That's a beauty! Must be some sort of dinosaur. The Museum would like that, I should think.'

Then he looked down at me and said, 'You'll be a lot more comfortable in the house, son.'

4 The Defence of the Weak

I ate hot buttered toast and strawberry jam until my fingers and chin were pleasantly greasy. My father was outside in the steamy sunlight. He had found an old scythe in the barn and he was sweeping it through the long grass which had once been a lawn. I could hear the swish of the big blade as it tore the grass down. My mother was washing brushes in the sink.

Neither of them had said anything to me. We'd talked, but nothing had been said about my day in the quarry. Nothing was said until I finished eating and my father came in, his shoes washed clean of clay by the wet grass.

He sat down across the table from me and he said, 'Saw you nip into the quarry this morning. Thought if you felt as strong as all that about it you'd be better not going to school.'

My mother wiped her hands on a painty towel and propped herself against the sink. 'Even if the shower hadn't come,' she said, 'we weren't going to have left you in the quarry all day.'

My father nodded. 'Didn't want to have you coming home and pretending you'd been at school.'

'I wouldn't have,' I muttered. 'I'd have told you.'

'We don't blame you, Jimmy,' my mother said. 'You just aren't the sort to fight, so the bullies will put on you. We don't blame you for being afraid to go to school.'

I stared at her. She was tall, like my father, but very slim and she looked young enough to be my sister. Sometimes she behaved like a sister. She was behaving like a sister now, tender and consoling, but not understanding the deep feelings that drove me.

'I wasn't *afraid*, Fiona!' I told her. 'Don't you see? I was just disgusted and ... and *mad*!'

My father nodded. 'Tell us about it, Jimmy.'

I tried, but how can you put revulsion and anger into words?

'Oh, I don't know. The whole place — that school, I mean — it's all wrong. It *feels* wrong. You'd expect a school to be a happy place, wouldn't you? It's full of kids and if kids aren't happy, who is? But Cronton isn't happy. It's hard and loud and nobody cares how anybody feels. That's why I stayed away. I wanted them to see how I feel about it.'

'You mean you aren't afraid of the bullies?' my mother asked.

' 'Course not, Fiona. They can't kill me. Anyway, I'm going to learn to fight and then they'll keep away from me. You've got to be able to fight. When I can I'll smash them up.'

'That's a horrible way of putting it,' she said.

I sniffed. 'That's how *they* put it.'

My father chuckled suddenly. 'So the school's a miserable dump? I think you've been a trifle hasty in your judgement — you've only put one day in — but if that's how you feel you're quite right to protest. But how are they going to know that you're protesting if you never go back? They'll think you were just scared and couldn't take it.'

It had already dawned on me that my protest would be flat unless people like Mr. Mason and Mr. Harris knew about it. What use was a protest nobody noticed?

'You'll have to go back, won't you?' my father said. 'You'll have to tell them why you stayed away today.'

I nodded. 'I'll tell them.'

My mother sighed and turned again to the sink. She said, 'I still think you should see the Head, John.'

'Not yet,' he said. 'Let Jimmy try it his way first. If his way doesn't work we'll all go and see the Head. But I think his way may work. And when you tell them, Jimmy, tell them also that we agree with you.'

'We agree with him,' my mother said, 'but one of us thinks that we're expecting too much. Tomorrow he'll have to face the teachers *and* the bullies.'

'I'll manage,' I said.

'I can help you with the bullies,' my father said.

I scowled at him. 'I don't want you coming to meet me, or anything like that.'

He shook his head. 'I don't mean that. Ever heard of judo?'

'I've heard of it. I've seen it on the telly. There's that woman who can chuck three or four men all over the place because she can do judo.'

'That's it, or something like it. If you knew judo you'd be able to throw the big boy — Fagso, do you call him? — all over the playground.'

I chuckled. 'That *would* be something!'

My mother had turned round again and she was watching my father. 'You aren't going to teach him judo, John?'

'Why not?'

'Because it's ... it's *physical*! It's brutal and violent.'

'It's scientific and beautiful, Fiona. We argued all this years ago and you won. But judo's the weapon of the weak against the strong. If everybody who was small or weak knew judo there'd be no more bullies.' My father looked at me and I saw the excitement in his eyes. 'I'll teach you judo, Jimmy!'

'Smashing!' I said. 'But who'll teach you!'

They both laughed. My father said, 'I know enough to teach you how to deal with Fagso. I did a bit at one time, before you were born. Started when I was a youngster. Went to the local gym and I got to be pretty useful.'

'John's a Black Belt,' my mother said.

Her voice and her eyes told me she was boasting about him. Just like her. She's always been so proud of my father that she boasts even when she doesn't approve of what he's done.

'What's a Black Belt?' I asked.

My father shrugged. He always shrugs off praise. 'It's just a belt, son.'

'It's the highest grade in judo,' my mother said. 'Beginners are White Belts and as they learn they go through a whole spectrum of belts and some of them

— a few, the very best — become Black Belts. John's one.' She swung back to the sink. 'Men are aggressive animals so they fight. If they must fight I suppose judo's the most civilized way. But it's still fighting.'

My father winked at me. 'Come on, son. I cut a patch of grass.'

'And I thought you were gardening,' my mother said.

We went out into the afternoon and my father loosened his big shoulders until I thought his clayey pullover must split.

'Breakfalls!' he said. 'First we'll learn breakfalls. Nothing matters if you don't know your breakfalls. They are ...'

He was talking to himself or to me or to anybody.

'What are breakfalls?' I asked him.

He threw himself backwards and sideways on to the ground yet, for all his size, he landed so lightly that he seemed barely to crush the grass. Then he rolled over and in a blur of movement he was on his feet.

'A breakfall!' he said. 'You've got to learn how to fall so that you don't damage yourself when you're thrown and so that you recover quickly. Try it, son.'

I fell backwards on to the ground with a crash that made the air whistle out of me and I lay, shaken, in the scent of damp earth and grass. I looked up at him. He was shaking his head.

'You didn't get it, Jimmy. Notice how I land on one arm and notice that I don't just land on it. I smash it against the ground. Watch again.'

This time he leapt backwards so that his body

went curving through the air and again he fell, just as lightly, so that he seemed hardly to touch the ground before he was up again.

'Got it?' he said. 'See how I hit the ground with my hand just before I fell? I really hit it. I smacked it hard. That way you absorb the shock. Try it.'

I tried again. I went on trying until I was gasping and dizzy and my legs were wobbly. My father never tired. Although he was more than twice my size he seemed to fall with less than half my weight and he barely disturbed the cut grass.

When my body was aching for rest my mother came out and said, 'Enough, John.'

We walked back to the house, his hand on my shoulder, and he talked quietly to me.

'We'll go on, son. We'll have another session tomorrow. We'll practise every day until you know how to deal with bullies without kicking them or smashing them up. That suit you?'

I nodded. A nod was about all I had strength for.

'Don't try any judo yet,' he said. 'On the bullies, I mean.'

My mother chuckled. 'He doesn't know any judo, John.'

'He doesn't know any *throws*,' he said, 'but he knows how to fall backwards and to the right and left. He's picked it up pretty quickly. But keep it to yourself, Jimmy. If you run into any trouble at school tomorrow . . . you're going tomorrow?'

I nodded.

'Keep your judo to yourself,' he went on, 'until I think you're ready. Then you'll give Fagso a surprise he'll never get over. But don't warn him what's coming. Don't mention judo and stay out of trouble.'

I couldn't stay out of trouble at Cronton. I was bound to generate trouble because I was different from the others there. I hadn't been schooled and drilled to fit into their pattern of behaviour: having never been part of a herd I didn't know the herd's laws.

I sat on the bus with Joe Belshaw. His face was glowing with morning shine and he met me with his slow grin.

'Bad yesterday.'

'What was bad?'

'You. You were bad 'cos you were away from school.'

'Ill?' I said. 'No, I was all right. I just didn't go to school.'

'Your mam let you stop at home, did she?'

'She didn't know. I just stayed.'

The two boys on the seat in front of us swung round. One of them was Ginger Evans, his tight waves shining like copper. The other was Midge Burnett, the smallest boy in 2E, and the most timid. He was a little mouse of a boy.

'You played wag!' Ginger Evans accused me.

'Truant?' I said. 'I suppose I did.'

He grinned. 'Bet you were too scared to come!'

'What was I scared of?'

He hooked his thumb at his chest. 'Me! That's who, mate!'

I felt sorry for him. He wanted more than anything to be tough, but he had to borrow the courage from somebody else. Nothing mattered much to Ginger so long as other boys were scared of him.

'You!' I said. 'You're pathetic! And I should be careful if I were you. Fagso's gang isn't here.'

Joe chuckled and Ginger said, 'I'll tell him! You wait till I tell Fagso!'

'One o' these days, Evans,' Joe growled deep in his chest, 'I'm going to smash you up so's your own mother won't know you!'

Anger flamed in Ginger's face. 'You, too, Belshaw! I'll tell Fagso! He'll do you at four!'

'He won't be doing anybody soon,' I said.

The glitter went out of Ginger's eyes. He couldn't understand me. He hated me because I was different.

'How d'you mean?' he asked.

My tongue had trapped me. I couldn't tell him about my judo.

'You'll see,' was all I could think of.

'Yah!' he jeered. 'You're all talk, big-head! Go on, clever! How are you going to stop Fagso? Nobody can stop Fagso. You taking boxing lessons, bighead?'

I had to think quickly of something. 'If we all stuck together,' I said, 'we'd stop Fagso. If all the kids in school, except his gang, stuck together we'd beat him.'

It sounded feeble enough to me, but Joe liked it. His face glowed with excitement.

'That's a beltin' idea! And we don't need all the school. Our Form'll be enough. Except you, Evans. We don't want you or any of the bob-a-week boys.'

Ginger was worried and angry. 'You wait, Belshaw! You just wait till four!'

'Why?' Joe asked. 'What will you do, sneaky Evans?'

'It's what Fagso'll do, mate. Not me. Fagso'll smash you up!'

'Not if we stick together,' I said. I looked at Midge Burnett, his big frightened eyes watching me over the back of the seat. 'How about you? Are you in?'

Midge blushed. 'I don't know. I never fight much.'

'Midge has got to be careful,' Joe said. 'He's got a weak heart or something and he doesn't do P.T. But there's Joss Hardy and Andy Phillips and Ticker Price and Bill Perks. They'd be enough, and I bet they'll come in.'

All Ginger could say was, 'You wait!'

I saw him before school in a playground corner with Nicker Edwards. Fagso wasn't there. He often came late. Ginger was talking so quickly that his face was red and Nicker was listening and nodding. He saw me and started across the playground, but the whistle blew and all he could do was shake his fist. For once I had avoided trouble.

I didn't avoid it for very long. We went into the hall and sat in uniformed rows of boys who stared at the rows of tired masters on the stage. I knew now what that nine o'clock whistle stood for. It stood for the end of naturalness and the beginning of restriction; boys restricted by discipline, masters restricted by necessity.

I was interested because it was all new to me. We sang a hymn and our lips said a prayer our minds didn't listen to and my thoughts went spinning along to find the reason for it all. It had nothing to do with learning or recreation so I guessed it must help the development of character. Then it was over, the masters were shuffling off the stage and the boys were snaking out through the door and my character felt no better at all. I decided that characters didn't get better quickly like a headache after an aspirin.

We went chattering along the corridor and into the classroom and there was Mr. Harris scowling at us. We sat down. He silently counted us, a brisk nod for each boy, and bent over his register. Beside me Joe Belshaw yawned.

I was wondering what made Mr. Harris so different from us. It wasn't age because I knew grown-ups who were just as human as kids. Mr. Harris was so different from us that he might have come from Mars. He was different because he wanted to be different; because he wanted us to feel that he was different; because . . .

He held out his hand towards me and said, 'Note, Stewart!'

I stopped wondering. I brought all my thoughts rushing back into my head and I said, 'Pardon?'

He sighed and looked at me. 'Sick-note, boy. You were absent yesterday.'

'I wasn't sick,' I said.

He straightened up slowly. 'Will you use the word "sir" when you speak to me, Stewart?'

I didn't see why I should. He hadn't got a title and he wasn't so terribly old. He wasn't Sir Charles Harris or an archbishop or anything like that. But I was trying to keep out of trouble so I said, 'I wasn't sick, sir.'

'Then why were you absent?' he asked.

This was what I had been waiting for. This was the moment I had made for myself.

'I played truant,' I said.

I saw him sway back on his heels and I felt the nervous gasp of the Form.

Mr. Harris said slowly, 'What will your parents say when they hear this?'

'They know, sir.'

'They found out?'

I nodded. 'They knew all the time.'

'And what did they say?'

'They said I was quite right, sir.'

He swayed back again until I thought he would topple. He was defeated. Nothing in his training or experience had prepared him for me. The boys were so silent that the air crackled.

'Did they?' Mr. Harris said, almost in a whisper. 'We'll go to the Head and see if he thinks you were quite right.'

Once again I trailed him like a shadow the whole length of the corridor and once again I waited outside the office while, inside, Mr. Harris talked of rebellion. He came out at last and, without even a glance at me, he said, 'Go inside.'

I went again through the lavender air of the secretary's room to the Headmaster's door. It was open. Mr. Mason, his whole length unfurled, was standing with his back to the gasfire.

'Come in, Stewart,' he said. 'And close the door.'

I could feel his blue eyes on me, penetrating more deeply than Mr. Harris's, stripping me of my composure and confidence.

'You played truant yesterday, Stewart,' he said.

'Yes, sir.'

'Why?'

'I didn't want to come.

'Why not?'

'I don't like the school.'

He nodded thoughtfully. 'There are times when I don't like it, Stewart, but I come nevertheless. I owe it to the boys to come. Do you owe it to anybody?'

'My parents, I suppose.'

'Oh, I don't know. Perhaps to some extent that's true. But most of all you owe it to yourself. To yourself, Stewart.' He stopped and looked at me hard, his eyes a little colder. 'You've been frank with me, Stewart. You tell me you don't like the school. Now I'm going to be frank with you. I'm not going to ask you what you don't like about the school because I don't think your opinion's of any value. You've been with us for one day. You haven't made any attempt to get to know us, yet you have the effrontery to say you don't like us. If that's how you feel you'd better leave us and let your parents go on educating you. If you decide to stay I don't want to see you at my door again. I'm too busy. There are six hundred boys in this school, Stewart, and every one of them is just as important as you are. Most of them are loyal to the school which you haven't yet learnt to be. All of them have been here long enough to become part of the school. Now go back to Mr. Harris, or go back home to your parents.'

I went back to Mr. Harris; back along the corridor feeling that I was a foot shorter; back into the classroom where my desk seemed to have grown too big for me.

Yet it was plain that in the eyes of the boys it was I who had grown. They examined me for signs of destruction and wrath and they found none. Once again I had defied Mr. Harris and braved the Head-master. Once again I had done something nobody else had done.

Mr. Harris was teaching English. He managed to teach without being aware that I was in the room. For me English meant a rich treasure of books; for Mr. Harris it meant parts of speech, phrases and clauses. That was the first time I'd ever disliked English.

During that day I found things in the school I didn't dislike. I found Gutsy Collins in the gym. He was a big bounding young man, dressed all in white, who made me feel that other lessons were no more than rests between gym periods. The boys liked him because he never asked any of them to do a thing he didn't first do himself and he never embarrassed the timid boys by making them do things they hadn't the courage for.

I wasn't one of the timid boys. I had the con-fidence that makes gymnastics easy and I enjoyed myself, balancing along benches and rolling over boxes. I even climbed one of the ropes, right to the ceiling, when I thought Gutsy wasn't watching. He was, and he slippered my backside, and in a way I enjoyed that, too.

Then in the afternoon there was Mr. Ferriby who taught Geography and who seemed to take me for a time to India so that I smelled the heat and the dust and almost wept over the thin cattle and thinner people. There was Pop Hawkins who taught Maths so casually and easily that difficulties disappeared before they became barriers.

At four o'clock I rushed out with everybody else in the race for home and at the gate I found Joe Belshaw.

'*Stew!*' he bellowed.

He had a crowd of boys with him — Joss Hardy, Andy Phillips, Ticker Price, Bill Perks and one or two more whose names I didn't know. Even Midge Burnett was there.

'Come on!' Joe said to me. 'Join the gang.'

'The anti-Fagso gang,' Joss Hardy said, grinning at me. 'We'll even have you in, big-head.'

'Pack it in, Hardy!' Joe growled. 'We've got to stick together. There's twelve of us. Like Stew said on the bus this morning if we stick together we can murder Fagso's boys.'

'There are thirteen of us,' I said.

Ticker Price looked darkly glum. He had only recently come to Cronton from a valley thrust high up the Welsh mountains where the villagers still believed in fairies.

'There's bad!' he said. 'Thirteen's unlucky, boy!'

'Thirteen?' Joe said, nodding his head at each of us in turn. 'You must be countin' Midge. You don't count him. He's here for protection. Now come on, and stick together and we'll murder Fagso's boys!'

But we didn't murder anybody. Nobody theatened us from the wood. It was a peaceful English wood with the afternoon sun slanting through the half-clad oaks and beeches. Our excitement evaporated in an instant and we felt that we had been cheated.

'There'll be another time,' Joe threatened, his breaking voice growling deeply.

So I went home and had an hour of judo on the cut-grass patch and I did my breakfalls so well that my father said I was ready for throws.

5 The Wrath of John

I practised judo every night that week. I learned hip-throws, back-throws, the cross-buttock. My father threw me about on the cut-grass patch until it began to look like an elephant's bed. Then on Friday I threw him and he sat on the grass, slowly rubbing one hand on the other, and he said, 'You're coming on, Jimmy.'

I learned more about school and I found that some of the masters were no longer stone-faced. Gutsy Collins wasn't. Neither was Pop Hawkins nor Dauber Dodge who taught Art and who quickly discovered some of my parents' talent in me.

On Friday we had Geography again and Mr Ferriby, still in India, mentioned fossils. I told him about my dragon.

'A dinosaur, Stewart?' he said. 'Where?'

I explained to him how a slab must recently have slipped from the back of the quarry and exposed the rock the dinosaur had died in.

'And you think it's a dinosaur,' he said. He held out a stick of red chalk. 'Show me. Do a sketch.'

I drew my dragon on the blackboard, as large as life and twice as fierce. I even made him breathe fire, red fire out of red jaws.

Mr. Ferriby chuckled and 2E grinned.

'Your imagination isn't fossilized, Stewart,' he said. 'I'll believe in your dinosaur when I see it.'

'It's right, sir,' Ginger Evans said from the back of the room. 'Nicker Edwards, out of 3R, he told me he'd been with Fagso Brown and they'd seen it. Nicker said it was painted on.' He pointed at me. 'Nicker said *he*'d painted it.'

'I did not!' I said.

Ginger snorted. Ginger didn't like me; never would like me. I'd taken away from him more than his desk.

'Bet you did!' he growled. 'Show off!'

'You can come and see for yourself,' I said to Mr. Ferriby.

He gave a nod. 'I'll do that. I'll be along tomorrow morning. If your dinosaur's genuine it's a very re-markable find.'

'It's painted!' Ginger grunted, but nobody took any notice of him and temper flamed in his face. He mouthed at me, '*You wait!*'

But nothing happened. Our little 2E army, a dozen boys united and invincible, marched down Holt Lane at four o'clock and when we reached the wood Fagso was there with Nicker Edwards and Ginger Evans. Fagso said nothing. He just smiled that little secret smile of his, but Nicker snarled, 'Big-head! Cockney big-head!' and Ginger screamed, 'Why d'you lot want to pal on with a Cockney big-head? You, Joe! You don't want a big-head for a mate!'

Our army halted and Joe Belshaw gave Ginger a long slow look and said, 'I don't want *you*, Evans!'

'You three'd best watch it!' Joss Hardy said. 'There's enough of us to beat you up.'

Fagso flicked a glance at him. 'You wanna try it, Hardy? You fancy yourself?'

'Not me!' Midge Burnett muttered. 'Come on! Let's go.'

'Not me either, boy!' Ticker Price said, shaking his head. 'I'm not mixing it with that lot; not until I've got to.'

'Clear off!' Fagso snarled. 'Go on, the lot of you, before I set into you!'

We walked in a tight bunch down the lane, silent at first, until Joss Hardy said, 'We beat 'em! They daren't tackle us! They were scared of us!'

But he was wrong and we all knew he was wrong. They were not afraid of us because Fagso, who was their courage, was afraid of nobody.

Midge Burnett shook his head. 'I don't know, Joss. We came away fast enough when Fagso told us to.'

'Good thing, too,' Ticker said.

The ugly screeching voice of Ginger Evans was chasing us along the lane. *'We've got a dragon in our garden! Big-head!'*

Joe chuckled. 'Fancy you having old Ferriby at your house tomorrow, Stew! You'll have to dress up in uniform.'

'Why?' I said.

'I wouldn't like it,' Andy Phillips said. 'Wouldn't have a teacher comin' to our house. You know what it's like in Admiral Street. They've been goin' to pull it down for years. I'd be ashamed.'

'What for?' Joss Hardy said. 'Your dad's as good as any teacher.'

66

'It isn't my dad,' Andy said. 'It's the house. It's so old.'

'It isn't as old as Stew's,' Joe said. 'My dad says Farley Farm's the oldest place for miles. Anyway, Ferriby isn't going to look at the house. It's that fossil he wants to see. Only a bloomin' teacher would want to see a fossil.'

'It's very interesting,' I said. 'You can all come if you feel like it.'

'Got me papers,' Joss Hardy said. 'By the time I've done the round I'm on my knees.'

'You're not getting me floggin' myself to death for a fossil,' Andy Phillips said. 'My bike's busted and I'd have to walk. It'd take me half an hour.'

'I'd like to see it,' Midge Burnett said. 'I've got some fossils at home, but not a dinosaur. I don't think I've ever seen a dinosaur.'

'I'll have to go if Midge goes,' Joe said, and then, to me, 'I sort of look after Midge. If I come, Stew, I'll have to bring our Gladys. My mam makes me take her with me when I go out Saturdays. I wish she'd get some pals of her own.' He glanced at Bill Perks. 'She'll be the only girl. How about your Molly, Bill? Will you be bringing her?'

Joss Hardy jeered and began to sing to the tune of *Three Blind Mice*, 'Joe loves Moll! He chased her over the fields one day . . .'

He squealed and sprang away when Joe, whose face was a beacon, swung on him.

'I'll do you, Hardy!' Joe muttered.

'It's the other way round at our house,' Bill Perks said. 'My mam makes our Molly take me with her when she goes out. I'm supposed to look after her.

My mam says you hear such things these days. You know, about girls being murdered. So I'll see you tomorrow, Joe, at Farley.'

'Round about ten o'clock,' I said.

Over tea I told my mother and father about Mr. Ferriby and the boys who were coming to see my dragon. They glanced at each other.

'It's an invasion,' my father said. 'Let's pray that it's peaceful.'

'It can't be,' my mother said. 'It's being led by one of the teachers from the school and we've been told what an unpleasant crowd they are.'

'Oh, Mr. Ferriby isn't so bad,' I said. 'He's human, I suppose. One or two of them are, as a matter of fact.'

They were pulling my leg and I knew that they were pleased.

It was late the next morning before I went to the quarry. First I practised judo. I didn't enjoy being thrown about on the wet grass but I had a cold determination to become so expert that I could show everybody that Fagso Brown was a brute who could be tamed. My father, who was already an expert, enjoyed the judo. He was more of a kid about it than I was. My mother didn't like it very much so she pretended that it wasn't going on.

My father taught me how to throw somebody who was attacking me from the front. When I rushed him he grabbed my sweater and rolled backwards, his foot pressed into my stomach, then, with a heave, he threw me. If he'd used his full strength he could have thrown me clean over the old fruit trees. Instead he threw me right across the cut-grass patch and I landed on my back and juggernauted into the young sycamores. By now I was using my breakfalls without having to think about them so, although I landed heavily enough, I wasn't hurt. I was just panting and dizzy.

'Now you do it to me,' my father said.

The first time I tried he went over me like a tank, but he kept me at it for half an hour until at last I threw him. It was surprising how easily I tossed him, big as he was, into the air. I heard him grunt as he hit the ground and I laughed.

'Again,' he said. 'You're still thinking about it. You've got to do it without thinking about it. It's got to be instinctive' — he grinned — 'like raising your hat when you meet a lady.'

I did it three more times before he was satisfied. He sat with his back to me, where I'd thrown him, and he said, 'You do that to Fagso and he'll think there's been an earthquake. But don't try it yet. Don't start thinking that you're good because you aren't. You're still doing it to numbers.' He stood up. 'I've got some clay to throw. What about you?'

I heard muffled laughter from the quarry and somebody squealed like a stoated rabbit.

My father nodded. 'Of course, you've got the invasion. Do you think it's started?'

'Sounds like it,' I said. 'I suppose Mr. Ferriby'll go to the house, John. I think he's like that; a bit polite. Tell him I'm in the quarry.'

I wanted to get to the quarry quickly. Somebody was throwing rocks about and the dull impact of rock on rock seemed to shake the earth. I was worried about my dragon.

My father, who often knew what my thoughts were before I could speak them, said, 'We'll both go, son.'

We hurried through the garden and into the quarry and there were Nicker Edwards and Fagso Brown throwing rocks at my dragon. I could see the sandy scars on the rock-face and the last rock, hurled just as we reached the quarry, hit the dragon's head and exploded all round it. Nicker's shout of triumph turned into a dismayed squeal when he spun round and saw my father coming up behind Fagso with the wrath of Jehovah in his eyes.

Nicker's face dropped and he yelled, 'Look out!'

But it was too late. My father's hand was already on Fagso's shoulder. Nicker ducked and went like a weasel out of the quarry.

Fagso turned to face my father and he refused to be afraid.

'You let me be, mate!' he rumbled. 'I'll fetch my old man!'

My father said nothing. His rages were rare and always silent. He took Fagso by the seat of his pants, and although Fagso kicked and struggled, he lifted him easily off the ground and laid him across his knee. Then he belaboured him. My father's hand could pick up a lump of clay which was a two-handed struggle for me and he brought this hand down on the drum-tight jeans across Fagso's back-side with a slap like cannon-fire. Time and again his hand came down until Fagso's roaring turned to sobbing and my father jerked him suddenly back to his feet. Fagso staggered. He was no longer the aggressive brute: he was a beaten little boy.

'You bring your old man,' my father said to him quietly. 'I'd like to see what sort of a father yours is.'

Fagso lumbered away without speaking and my father sent a sad smile after him.

'I didn't enjoy that very much,' he said. 'Neither did Fagso. I hope it'll do him some good.' He took a deep breath and straightened himself up. 'Time for me to start throwing that clay.'

I had the whole quarry to myself, but I was interested only in my dragon and his scars. I reached up on tip-toe and with my hand carefully wiped his old bones. My foot groped for the jumble of fallen rocks so that I could reach higher. It found nothing. The rocks had been moved and where they had lain were flattened patches of sickly grass, like a fungus growth. Then I saw that the little cave had gone, its mouth hidden behind the rocks somebody had piled in front of it.

I rolled one rock away and I heard a sound, a voice that squeaked and trembled hollowly, and I realized that I had heard the sound through all the long seconds after my father had gone but had not listened to it, so great were my fears for my dragon. I pulled another rock aside and I saw a little face shining out of the cave's darkness. I heaved at the biggest rock, but it was heavy and coated with soil.

'Let me out!' piped the voice.

I gave another heave, the best I had, and the rock moved enough for Midge Burnett to scuttle out into

71

the daylight. Still on hands and knees he looked up at me and his eyes were enormous.

'I struck matches!' he said.

'Who did it?' I asked him. 'Fagso and Nicker Edwards? Did they put you in there?'

I wouldn't have thought that so small a body could have held so much terror. He was shaking.

'*Gelignite!*' he whispered. 'In there! I struck matches!'

I sat on the biggest rock and I ground my teeth together. 'It's time somebody settled with Fagso Brown! You should have seen what my father did to him, but it needs a kid to settle him properly.'

Midge was nodding like a doll. 'I saw! I peeped through a crack! There's a box in there with sticks of gelignite in it! They're fused!'

'Gelignite?' I asked.

'I keep telling you. It's in there. I found the box and I thought it was treasure and I struck matches.' A great shudder shook him. 'I could have been blown up! If I'd dropped that match ...'

'Gelignite?' I said again. 'That's explosive, isn't it?'

' 'Course it is! There are four sticks with a fuse fastened to them ...'

'Is the fuse the thing like wire?'

'You've seen it already? You've been in there?'

I nodded. 'I haven't actually seen it. I felt it. I went in there the day I played truant. Gelignite's dangerous, isn't it?'

He shuddered again. 'I'll say! I'll bet it could blow this hill away. I'll bet it's been there since they stopped quarrying two or three years ago. You want to tell your dad. You want to get the police . . .'

His voice trailed away and he scrambled to his feet. My mother and father were coming into the quarry with Mr. Ferriby walking between them. He didn't look a bit like a teacher. He was wearing a thick sweater and there was a pipe in his mouth. I remember noticing that he was holding it, self-consciously clenched, as if he was only learning to smoke it.

'How lovely!' my mother said. 'Savage and beautiful!'

She was staring at my dragon and I felt proud that it was mine.

Mr. Ferriby took the pipe out of his mouth and said, 'I don't believe it!'

My father grinned at little Midge and winked at me. 'Is this the invasion?' he asked.

'Part of it,' I said. 'Midge Burnett.'

Midge's head rolled back as he looked up at my father. 'I saw you belt Fagso Brown, Mr. Stewart. I laughed like mad even if I was scared.'

'What had you to be scared of?' my father said.

Midge pointed at the cave. 'I was in there, in the dark. They pushed me in and fastened it up with stones. I was glad you belted him.'

'So am I now,' my father said. 'Fagso wasn't very pleased.'

I was watching Mr. Ferriby and wondering how long it would be before he believed in my dragon. He was standing on the biggest rock to examine it, his fingers stroking and his eyes scanning.

'It's true!' he said. 'It's real!'

'It's mine!' I said.

He didn't hear me. Nobody heard me. His excitement was making my mother and father excited. At last he stepped down and put his forgotten pipe into his mouth.

'It's the first time I've seen it,' my mother said. 'I remember Jimmy mentioned it. It's a beautiful thing.'

'It's astonishing,' Mr. Ferriby said.

'Is it in some way important?' my father asked him.

Mr. Ferriby removed his pipe again. He hadn't learnt to talk with it between his teeth. 'I'm no geologist, but I'll bet a year's salary that there hasn't been a geological find like it in Britain in this century. It's a dinosaur, of course, but I don't know which species. We really ought to get the Professor on to it. He's a world authority. It should go to the Museum, Mr. Stewart. Any objections?'

My father shrugged. 'You'd better see the chap who owns the quarry. His name's Thwaites.'

'I know him,' Mr. Ferriby said. 'He'll be all right. I'll get on to the Museum right away. They'll probably send somebody tomorrow. The whole slab'll have to be cut out, you see. It's a tricky job.'

'You can phone from the house,' my father said.

Mr. Ferriby nodded. 'Fine! I'd like to get on with it right away. I hope all this won't be a nuisance to you, Mrs. Stewart. Geological fame's about to descend on Farley.'

My mother was studying the dragon. She had no interest in it as a dinosaur, alive or dead. To her it was an arrangement of lines, savagely and beautifully sketched.

'I'll use it in a design, John,' she said. 'We'll make it the trade-mark of Farley Ware.'

They walked out of the quarry and through the fruit trees towards the house, talking all the time, but none of their talk was for me. They never thought that it was I who had found the dragon: they never acknowledged that it was my dragon; that they had seen it only because I had told them about it. All their talk was of the plans they had for carting my dragon away, for displaying it, for painting it on pots. They were too grown up to remember for a moment that a kid had found it and thought he owned it.

'He's O.K. is Mr. Ferriby,' Midge said. 'Why didn't you tell your dad about the gelignite?'

'He isn't having it!' I said.

Midge's young–old face wrinkled. 'Who isn't?'

'Ferriby! That's who!'

'I don't suppose he wants it.'

I glared at Midge. 'You heard him, didn't you? He's going to tell them to cut it out and take it to the Museum.'

'I was talking about the gelignite,' Midge murmured.

'I wasn't! I'm talking about my dragon.' Inside me there was a volcano of resentment and jealousy. 'It isn't going to any museum! It's mine and it's staying here!'

'How can you stop them?'

I didn't know. What hope had my kid's anger of penetrating the smugness of grown-ups?

'I'll stop them!' I said, furiously thinking. 'It's mine! Before I'll let them take it away I'll . . .'

'I think you ought to tell your dad about the gelignite,' Midge muttered.

'I'll blow it up!' I shouted.

Midge's little face was all eyes. I turned away from his fear. Somebody was coming into the quarry.

6 Explosion

Joe Belshaw, grinning like a chimpanzee, was coming into the quarry with a girl. He pushed the brambles aside for her and trod down the long grass for her and I thought at first when I saw her she was worth all his fussing. She was about the prettiest girl I'd ever seen. She was so pretty that looking at her made my chest ache.

'Molly Perks!' Midge whispered.

Behind them walked Bill Perks, fed up and glowering, with another girl, a younger, smaller girl whose face was a freckled replica of Joe's.

'Gladys Belshaw!' Midge whispered.

I thought it was a pity she had to be with Molly Perks. It was like putting fine porcelain beside terracotta. The one made the other awkward and ugly. Molly Perks, I suppose, would have made most girls look awkward and ugly.

'Mean to say we've flogged it all the way here to look at that!' Bill Perks growled.

He was glaring at my dragon. The sight of Molly Perks had drugged me into forgetfulness so that I had forgotten my dragon and my anger and resentment.

'Nobody made you come!' Molly flashed at him.

She had a porcelain voice, smooth and hard. She turned to me. 'Our Bill told me about you. He says you're funny.'

I felt about as funny as a wet Saturday. I'd never seen eyes with lashes so long as hers. When she closed them my heart leapt into my throat.

Joe chuckled. 'You can say that again, Molly! You want to ask Charlie Harris how funny Stew is.'

He was trying to be posh. His face was scrubbed and his hair watered down and I knew how he felt. Already, after only two minutes with her, my hands seemed rough and my face dirty.

'I think it's nice,' Gladys said. 'What is it?'

She was standing with her legs astride and her hands clasped behind her and she was looking up at my dragon. Midge Burnett came suddenly to life.

'It's a fossil,' he said. 'It's a dinosaur. Mr. Ferriby's been and he wants it.'

'He can have it for me,' Bill said.

Midge shook his head. 'He can't. It's Stew's.'

This brought all their eyes back to me, but I was conscious only of Molly's. I had known no more than a couple of girls in my life — my cousins — and Molly made them something less than girls.

'Did he buy it?' Bill asked. He was bad-tempered and prickly. 'Did you buy that thing, Stewart? Did you buy old Thwaites's quarry?'

'I found it,' I said.

'Finding's keeping,' Joe said.

'He's going to blow it up!' Midge said.

Joe had picked up a stone to throw; Bill was wandering away: Gladys was trying to balance, like Eros, on a rock. Midge's words stopped all of them.

'Blow it up!' Joe said. 'You're nuts!'

Midge nodded violently. 'Stew said he'd blow it up!'

Bill looked at me. 'It's you that's nuts!'

'You've nothing to blow it up with,' Joe said.

'He's got gelignite,' Midge said. 'I found four sticks in that little cave.' He was enjoying himself. Never in his life had he so impressed boys bigger and stronger than himself. 'One of the sticks has got a fuse on it.'

Joe scowled at him. 'What were you doin' in that cave? Eh? It's damp in there, I bet. You're supposed to keep out of the damp. You know what your mam told you. You've had rheumatic fever once and you don't want it again.'

Midge blushed and said in a whisper, 'It was Fagso and Nicker.'

'They were here early,' I said. 'They pushed him in there and closed it up with rocks . . .'

'Why didn't you stop them?' Joe growled.

Midge, remembering another excitement, found his voice again. 'It was before Stew got here. He didn't know I was in there and he came with his dad when Fagso and Nicker were throwing stones at the fossil and Stew's dad didn't half belt Fagso. You should have seen it!' He hugged himself. 'I bet nobody ever belted Fagso like that.'

They stared at me while he told the story, turning every blow of my father's hand into a thunder-clap. Gladys squealed and danced.

Joe said, 'I wish I'd seen it. Never seen anybody

clout Fagso. That's what Fagso wants — cloutin'. Wish there was a kid could do it. Wish I could do it.'

Bill took a deep breath. 'Fagso'll tell his dad and he'll come here and he'll *do* your dad, Stew. He's no good, Fagso's dad. He gets drunk and he swears. He clouts Fagso a lot, but he won't let anybody else. Your dad had best watch out.'

'You've never seen Stew's dad,' Midge said, his eyes open wide. 'He's a giant. He picked Fagso up with one hand and clouted him. When Fagso cleared off he was *crying*!'

Gladys squealed again. Molly wasn't enjoying this very much. She liked everybody to look at her. She started to hum a tune and sway her hips.

'After Mr. Stewart had gone,' Midge said, 'Stew found me in the cave and let me out. Then, after a bit, he came back — Mr. Stewart, I mean — with Stew's mam and Mr. Ferriby. After he'd had a good look at Stew's fossil Mr. Ferriby went off to phone some museum to get them to take it away and Stew says they can't 'cos it's his.'

'Why's it yours any more than Ferriby's?' Bill asked me.

'I found it,' I said. 'He would never have known about it if I hadn't told him.'

Joe nodded. 'That's right. You told him and he didn't believe you.'

'And he never even spoke to Stew,' Midge said. 'He had a look at the fossil and then said it'd have to be taken away. He said it was very important: it would make Farley famous.'

Joe snorted. 'It'll make him famous, I bet.'

'And he never mentioned that Stew found it,' Midge said.

'Never will,' Joe said. 'He'll say he found it and they'll call it a fancy name and his picture'll be in the papers.'

'Just like a teacher!' Bill said. 'The kids do all the work and they get all the credit. It's always the same.'

'So Stew says they aren't having it,' Midge said. 'He says it's his and if anybody wants it they should ask him.'

' 'Course they should!' Joe said. 'What do you expect of adults?' He was scowling. He was feeling so angry that he had forgotten Molly Perks. Everybody had forgotten her.

She gave a loud sniff. 'You talk like a bunch of kids! What can you do about it?'

'Blow it up,' Midge said. 'That's what Stew says.'

She tossed her head. 'Talk! He daren't do it.'

'Stew'll do it,' Midge said. 'He told me he was going to, so he will. He wasn't even scared of old Harris.'

'He wouldn't have the nerve!' she said, and I hated her. 'He'd be petrified!'

I was making for the cave. I plunged into it, crawled blindly along until my fingers gripped the edge of the box and I dragged it out into the daylight. The others were waiting for me. They crowded round and in silence studied the four greasy sticks that lay in the bottom of the box. Beside them was a thick coil of fuse.

'It's wicked!' Gladys said.

'Best leave it, kid,' Joe said. 'That stuff's dangerous. You read about kids who find explosives and blow themselves to bits.'

'It doesn't look so dangerous to me,' Bill said. 'How do we know it's explosive? Who said it was?'

'Me,' Midge said. 'It's got "Danger" on the side of the box, so it must be explosive.'

Molly sniffed and Bill said, 'Why? Could be something else, couldn't it?'

'Don't talk wet!' Joe said. 'They wouldn't put "Danger" on the box if it was corned beef, would they?'

'Corned beef can be dangerous,' Midge said. 'My mam won't let us eat it. She says people have died through eating corned beef.'

Joe pointed. 'That isn't corned beef! It's explosive! It's that gelignite stuff.'

'How do you set it off?' I asked.

'You light that fuse,' Midge said. 'You light it at the end.'

'Then you run like 'ell!' Bill said, and Gladys scowled at him.

'I don't think you should, Jimmy Stewart,' she said.

Molly smirked. 'I don't think he *dare*!'

I uncoiled the fuse. There must have been six or seven feet of it. I laid it on the ground and piled rocks in front of the cave until the box was hidden and only the fuse, dead and harmless in the grass, was still showing. Nobody helped me. The others stood silently round and watched me as I worked.

'Lend me your matches,' I said to Midge.

I struck one and Molly said, 'He's daft! He ought to be in a home!'

Bill gave a little frightened laugh. 'I'm off!' he said.

I held the end of the fuse in the flame until my fingers were scorched, but nothing happened.

'I wonder how you know when it's burning,' I said.

'It sort of splutters,' Midge said. 'I saw it on the telly.'

'Well this stuff won't splutter,' I said. 'It must be damp or old or something.'

'I knew you'd find some excuse!' Molly called.

I glanced back over my shoulder. She was standing with Joe about twenty yards away. His arm was round her shoulders and she was wilting against him. I knew then why I didn't like her. At first I'd seen only her prettiness, but now I saw that her blue eyes were mean and her lips, red and fresh, were pulled down in the sneer that was part of her.

'Why don't you go away!' I said to her.

'I think you shouldn't do it, Jimmy Stewart,' Gladys said.

She was standing on one side of me. Midge Burnett, waiting for his matches, was on the other.

He said, 'I think you're supposed to blow on it.'

'You come here, our kid!' Joe called.

Gladys ignored him. I looked up at her, at the freckled concern on her face, and I grinned.

'I don't think you should,' she told me again.

By now I didn't think I should, but again I saw Molly's chilly sneer and I said, 'I'm going to. You two kids had better get out of the way.'

They left me. I was alone and afraid and no longer angry. I glanced up at my dragon. They wanted to rip his fifty-million-year fury out of the rock to decorate a museum. They were going to take his red-lined shape in a slab and stick a number on it and give it a fancy name. But he was mine. Grown-ups weren't going to steal him and own him and never say a word to me who had found him.

I struck another match. The scrape of its head on the box thundered round the quarry and its flame licked at the fuse. I blew on it and suddenly there was a splutter of sparks. I dropped the fuse and I ran.

The others fled in front of me like sheep before a wolf. They stampeded out of the quarry and round the side of the hill and I caught them and we stood together in a tight trembling cluster. Gladys pressed her fists into her ears: Molly's lips were as pale as her cheeks: Joe looked troubled: Bill giggled and said, 'Blasting!'

'Let's get farther away!' Midge whispered.

Nobody bothered about Midge. He dashed a few yards down the slope, stopped, and then came back to the comfort of our closeness.

'You shouldn't have done it, Jimmy Stewart,' Gladys said. Her eyes were screwed up, but her voice accused me.

'You wait till I tell!' Molly said.

I knew that Gladys was right and that, although she was the youngest of us, she understood better than any of us the wrongness of what I had done. Her child's wisdom told her that my dinosaur had not been preserved through the ages to be blown to dust because of a kid's anger and jealousy.

'It's takin' some time,' Bill said.

'You never lit it!' Molly said. Her sneer was more acid than ever. 'You were only pretending! I knew you'd be scared!'

Gladys opened her eyes and smiled at me. 'I'm glad you didn't do it.'

But I knew the fuse would still be burning, its little fire spluttering closer to the explosive. I knew that at any moment my dinosaur would fly into a thousand fragments.

I spun round and started running. My feet seemed to drag through the grass and although I was panting and straining I wasn't moving fast enough to make a breeze in my face. The journey back to the quarry was a daylight nightmare in which I ran until my heart was thudding against my ribs and yet I seemed scarcely to be moving. At last I turned into the quarry and I saw my dragon still snarling in the rock, and the tiny curl of smoke that floated in front of the cave entrance. I tried to spurt forward, but just then the cave erupted red flame and smoke, my dragon jerked and slipped, the air was filled with flying things and I was picked up by a rush of heat and hurled backwards into the grass.

I don't remember hearing the explosion. All I remember is the tattoo of rocks falling back to earth and ripping through branches. I remember the devil's smell the breeze brought me, a smell of fire and smouldering. I remember the dust in the air, lit up by the sun shafting over the edge of the quarry. The noises stopped and I went on lying in a great silence until somebody came running towards me and somebody said, '*He's dead!*'

I sat up. Joe and Bill were there and so was

Gladys, so pale that the freckles splashed over her face seemed to have multiplied. Molly wasn't there with her sneer.

'Where's Molly?' I asked.

'Cleared off,' Bill said. 'Just like a girl!'

'I'm a girl,' Gladys said and sounded like a woman. She looked at me. 'Are you all right, Jimmy Stewart?'

I nodded. Midge was creeping into the quarry, his nose, like a mouse's, twitching nervously. He looked so funny that I wanted to laugh, but I didn't. Other people were coming in a rush. My father was first, bursting like a tank through the fruit trees. Behind him came my mother and Mr. Ferriby. I climbed to my feet.

'You all right, son?' my father called.

I nodded.

'Did somebody drop a bomb?' my mother asked.

Joe and Bill and Gladys and Midge stood tight-lipped. Not even gelignite could have forced the story out of them. Mr. Ferriby went to the rock-face where the dragon had once been. It had vanished. The cave was still there, but above it the cliff was clean and new where rock had been wrenched away.

'It was explosive,' I said. 'Gelignite or dynamite or something. I found it in a box at the end of the cave. I set it off.'

My mother blew out a long breath and my father said, 'A bit early for November the fifth, son.'

My mother started to push the hair off my forehead and when that was done she tried to slap the dust from my clothes.

I said, 'Don't, Fiona. I'm all right.'

'All right!' she said, still slapping, and now I wasn't sure whether she was slapping my clothes or me. 'I thought you'd have had more sense than muck about with explosive.'

I stepped away from her. 'I wasn't mucking about! I set it off on purpose.'

My father was watching me, reading my thoughts again. 'I should think you'd a pretty good reason.'

Mr. Ferriby was shaking his head as if there could be no reason good enough.

I nodded at him. 'It was so that he couldn't take my dragon away . . . the fossil, I mean.'

'And you thought . . .' my mother started to say, but my father's eyes stopped her.

'Seems a bit short-sighted, Jimmy,' he said to me.

'I found that fossil, John, and I called it mine. You and Fiona came with Mr. Ferriby and you talked about it and you decided that it had to go to the Museum and you never said anything to me. You never asked me, and I'd found it, so I blew it up!'

'Rather selfish,' my mother said.

My father nodded. 'We were, Fiona. Very selfish. Thoughtless, too.'

Mr. Ferriby put his hand on my shoulder. 'Come and have a look, Jimmy,' he said.

I went with him to the cave where the devil's smell was so strong that it tickled my nose. He pointed and there was my dragon, still in the slab of rock which had held him for so long. It had fallen and was now propped against the rock-face.

'It isn't damaged,' he said. He picked up a rock as big as a football and raised it in both hands above his head. 'I'll smash it for you.'

He was odd. Like all grown-ups he did pointless things.

'What for?' I almost shouted at him.

I saw his eyes swivel to look at me.

'It's your fossil,' he said. 'You found it and you don't want anybody else to have it so I'll smash it up for you. Or would you rather do it yourself?'

This time I did shout at him. 'No! Nobody's going to smash it!' Then, quietly, I said, 'It's going to the Museum!'

My father was sitting on a rock. He chuckled. 'They'll probably name it after you, Jimmy.'

'So they should,' my mother said. 'He found it and he removed it from the rock.'

'And scared the wits out of everybody within a mile,' my father said.

Then there was another voice, a strange coarse voice like a file on hard metal. 'Where's the bloke that clouted our Raymond?'

I spun round. There was a man behind us in the quarry. I'd never seen him before but I knew him. I knew him because Fagso had his thick lips and little eyes and because Fagso and Nicker, come for vengeance, were watching from the fruit trees. He was Fagso's father, as savage and brutal as Fagso.

'I'm lookin' for the bloke that clouted our Raymond!' he growled.

So Fagso's name was Raymond! That was the funniest thing in a funny morning and I laughed. Mr. Brown turned his eyes slowly on me so that I could see how mean and bloodshot they were.

'What you laughin' at, kid?'

'He could be laughing at you,' my father said.

Mr. Brown's eyes moved, still slowly, to my father. 'And who're you?'

'I'm the bloke who clouted your Raymond,' my father said.

Mr. Brown grunted. 'So you're the bloke I'm lookin' for!'

'And now you've found me,' my father said.

He stood up. He was behind me, but I knew he was standing up because I saw Mr. Brown's eyes follow him and I saw them change. I saw all the bully's bravado, all the brutishness fade out of them until there was no more menace in them than in the eyes of a kicked dog. I didn't look at my father but I knew he was standing up, a tower of a man, quiet and calm and smiling.

He pointed at Fagso, still waiting under the trees with Nicker for a massacre. 'If that's Raymond I smacked him,' he said. 'And who are you?'

'I'm Raymond's dad, mister,' Mr. Brown said in a cringing voice. 'Thought I'd come and see what was what, sort of.'

'And what is what?' my father asked.

'Just thought I'd find out why you'd clouted him, mister. What he'd been up to, sort of.'

'He'd been up to vandalism,' my father said, 'and I gave him what's good for vandals.'

'And he pushed Midge in the cave,' Gladys piped up, 'and he fastened him in so's Midge couldn't get out.'

Midge started to blush.

'And Midge's got to be careful,' Joe said. 'He's got a bad heart.'

'Shurrup!' Midge muttered.

'Do 'im, Dad!' Fagso called from the trees.

Mr. Brown, finding something safe to turn his anger on, swung round. 'I'll do *you*, me lad, when I lays me hands on you!' He turned back to my father. 'Sorry you've been troubled, mister.'

'No trouble at all,' my father said.

Mr. Brown was nodding like a donkey, his final nod almost a bow. He stalked after Fagso who was running with Nicker through the trees.

My mother made the snarling noise she makes when a design won't come right. 'What a brute! I was hoping he'd go for you, John, so that you could deal with him.'

My father grinned and put his arm round her shoulders and hugged her. 'And this is the woman who hates violence! The woman who says that men are aggressive!'

'That man,' my mother said, 'is the sort who only understands violence.'

'I'm glad it was you, and not me, he was looking for,' Mr. Ferriby said.

My father shook his head. 'He wouldn't have done a thing. He's all bluster. Poor Fagso! That boy's never stood a chance.'

7 The Life-saver

They came in a van on Sunday afternoon and took my dragon away. They backed the van as near as they could to the quarry where my father and Mr. Ferriby were waiting for them.

There were four men in the van. One of them was old, older than my father or Mr. Ferriby or any of the others, but his eyes were bright and young and his skin had the soft pinkness of a baby's. He looked at the dinosaur for a long time and then he told me that I was lucky to have found it and clever to have known what it was.

'I think it's new,' he said. 'New or not, it's never been found in Europe before and that makes it important.'

He watched the men wrap the dinosaur slab in sheets of thick cloth. Mr. Ferriby said to him, 'If it's new, Professor, you'll name it, of course?'

The old man nodded. I was near to him now and I could see that the pinkness of his face was really the transparency of the skin which looked almost too fragile to touch.

'I'll name it,' he said, chuckling. 'I'll name it for its discoverer. *Ornithomimus stewarti!*' He chuckled again, so hard that his cheek-pouches wobbled.

They carried my dragon to the van and loaded it

so carefully it might have been shattery Dresden, and then they drove away. I stayed in the quarry on my own for a time, but it wasn't the same. It seemed empty. They had taken away more than a slab of rock and the tracery of old bones. They had taken an excitement, a feeling that the quarry was a special place, a place a kid could have secrets in. Even the cave was different. It was now only a hole with blast-marks sprayed on the rock all round it.

So I went back to the house and found my father and mother showing pots to Mr. Ferriby. They didn't even notice me. I was fed up and I caught myself looking forward to school the next day; looking forward to seeing the boys again and to hearing the kids' chatter about my father's quiet victory over Mr. Brown.

Yet I found as soon as I reached school on the Monday morning that there was another excitement, a fresh hero. Midge Burnett had fallen into the canal on Sunday afternoon and Joe Belshaw had dived in to save him. Midge couldn't swim: Joe could.

Joe told us about it before school. A swarm of worshipping First-Year boys buzzed round him in a corner of the playground while I hovered on the fringe to listen.

'Went fishing with our Gladys. Midge said he'd come, but he was late. I started fishing near that bend where the old railway is and our kid sat behind me. Only been fishing a bit when Bill Perks rolled up . . .'

'Bet their Molly was with him!' somebody shouted.

Joe blushed. 'Bill said Midge was behind them, coming along the towpath . . .'

'We'd seen him,' Bill said. 'I wanted to wait, but our kid wouldn't. She's got a new transistor and she wanted to show it to Gladys Belshaw. Midge was a heck of a way behind us and there was a gang of kids following him.'

'Midge never came,' Joe said. 'It was a long time after Bill came and our kid and Molly Perks had gone off along the towpath 'cos the transistor was scaring the fish away, and we heard a shout, all gurgly and scared. We ran like mad and there was Midge, right out in the middle of the canal and he isn't even supposed to get his feet wet.'

'Joe never stopped,' Bill said, proud to have been there. 'He went straight in like a bomb and he got Midge, turned him on his back and life-saved him just like in the baths. I pulled him out — Midge, not Joe — and got him on the towpath. He was O.K. He was scared and crying a bit, but he was O.K. I wanted to give him the kiss of life, but he wouldn't let me 'cos he wasn't dead.'

'What about the other kids?' somebody asked. It was Specky Miller, my first tormentor.

'What other kids?' Bill asked him.

'You know! The *other* kids! You said there was a gang of kids behind Midge.'

Bill shrugged. 'Never saw them after we got Midge out. They must have cleared off.'

'Funny!' Specky said, looking owlishly wise at the rest of us. 'Wonder where they'd gone? Wonder who they were?'

'Dunno,' Bill said. 'They were too far away. One

of them was a red-haired kid and another was big.'

'As big as Fagso Brown?' Specky asked.

Bill was saying, 'Could be,' when Fagso pushed through the crowd, scattering the little First Years like leaves. He grabbed Specky by the ear.

'You talkin' about me, young Miller?'

Specky squealed and wriggled. 'No, Fagso! We was talkin' about Midge Burnett; about him fallin' in the canal and Joe Belshaw pullin' him out!'

Fagso gave the ear a twist. 'I heard you, young Miller! You were on about me!'

Specky's eyes filled with tears, huge drops seen through his thick lenses. 'There was some other kids there and they cleared off. One of them was a big kid!'

'Wasn't me!' Fagso said.

' 'Course it wasn't!' Specky howled. 'You're hurting my ear, Fagso! I brought my bob. It's in my pocket. You can have it now, if you want.'

I said, 'Leave him alone!'

Fagso pushed Specky away and turned round. The First-Year boys near to me dodged to safety.

'You brought your old man?' Fagso asked me.

'I don't need him,' I said. Suddenly Joe Belshaw was on one side of me and Bill Perks on the other. Joss Hardy and Ticker Price were there, too.

'You better not try fighting all of us, Fagso!' Joe said.

'You try it, boy,' Ticker said, 'and you'll think the wall fell on you.'

'How's your backside, Fagso?' Bill asked. 'Think you'll be able to sit down?'

Somebody giggled. So furious was Fagso's rage that I thought it must explode out of him. He was a bully yet I knew he had an unthinking, animal courage, and for a second I thought he was going to rush us. I wondered if I could remember my judo. Then the duty master's whistle blew away the tension and Fagso's body loosened and he pushed his hands into his pockets.

'I got plans for you kids!' he said.

Mr. Harris was late coming down from the hall and the excitement in 2E was electric. Joe and I, sitting together at the front, were put through a catechism which made me dizzy.

'Tell us about your dad, Stew! Tell us how he clouted Fagso's dad!'

'He didn't!'

'What did you blow old Ferriby up for?'

'I didn't!'

'I bet you'll be in court, Stew, for setting dynamite off!'

'I shan't!'

'Where did you pinch the dynamite from?'

'I didn't!'

'Think they'll give you a medal, Joe? For saving Midge?'

Joe scowled. 'The kids who were behind him won't get a medal, I bet.'

'They must have seen him! Who were they?'

'How would I know? I never saw them!'

'One was a red-headed kid,' Bill Perks said. Everybody turned to Ginger Evans, sulking at the back of the room. Bill went on, 'He was about your size, Evans.'

Ginger, spotlighted by thirty pairs of eyes, blushed until his hair and face were all one.

'Well it wasn't me! I never went out yesterday. You can ask my dad.'

'I saw you, boy,' Ticker said in his quiet Welsh tones. 'You went along our street round about two o'clock.'

Ginger snarled. 'I went for some fags for my dad. You ask him.'

'*Charlie!*' somebody whispered and silence filled the room like magic.

Mr. Harris came in. He walked to his desk, saying without looking at them, 'Belshaw and Perks! the Headmaster wants you.'

Joe and Bill, worried in an instant, their minds searching for something they were guilty of, walked into the corridor.

Mr. Harris opened his register. 'And how's Blaster Stewart this morning?'

There was a titter which swelled into a laugh. In one second he had given me the name which was to be mine right through school. He glanced up at me.

'Brought any high explosive with you this morning?'

There was another, louder laugh. I said, 'No, Mr. Harris.'

He frowned and turned again to his register and said, 'Burnett's absent. He went swimming yesterday, I hear.'

It was another joke, but this time nobody laughed. Midge was too small, too insubstantial to be funny.

There wasn't a chance until dinnertime to find out why Mr. Mason had wanted Joe and Bill. They didn't come back to us until after Break and by then we were having French and Mr. Dillon didn't allow any English whispering. As soon as we were in the dining-hall Joss Hardy said, 'What did he want, Joe? Did he stick you?'

Joe gave a lofty smile and said nothing until grace was finished. I chanted it with the rest of them.

'For what we are about to receive . . .'

I looked at my plate. Potatoes, soggily mashed, and two pale sausages. I supposed it was a good thing to give thanks even for the smallest blessings. I had heard of children starving in India.

We sat down to a scraping of chairs and the rattle of cutlery on formica tops.

'Come on, Joe!' Joss said. 'Tell us! You want to know, don't you, Blaster?'

I said nothing.

Joe winked at Bill Perks, across the dining-hall, and said to us, 'Midge's dad was there with old Mason. Wanted to thank us for saving young Midge.'

' "Us?" ' Joss said. 'It was you, Joe.'

'Bill gave me a hand,' Joe said. 'I'd have had some job getting Midge up the bank if Bill hadn't been there.'

'And what did old Mason say?' somebody asked.

'The Headmaster and me, we had a little chat,' Joe said. 'A bit of a discussion, you might call it.'

He stopped and Joss clattered his fork on the table. 'What did he want to know?'

'Who those other kids were,' Joe said, suddenly

serious. 'The ones Bill saw behind Midge. We couldn't tell him.'

'Why couldn't you?' Ticker Price asked him.

' 'Cos we didn't know, that's why. I'd never seen them and they were so far away when Bill saw them he couldn't make them out.'

Joss snorted. 'Why do they matter, anyway?'

'They matter,' Joe said slowly, ' 'cos they chucked Midge in.'

That stopped everybody eating. Even I, to whom other boys were still an unending surprise, stopped chewing and swallowed hot sausage.

'Nobody would do *that*!' I said.

Joe flicked a glance at me. 'They did. Those kids chucked Midge in. Midge says so and he isn't a liar.'

'Midge ought to know them,' Andy Phillips said.

Joe shrugged. 'He told his dad he'd never seen them before. He says he didn't really see them yesterday. They came up behind him and gave him a push. He says they probably didn't know he can't swim. As soon as they'd knocked him in they went running off across the field towards Farmer Mosedale's wood. That's what Midge told his dad.'

'There's some bad kids come out here from Grimthorpe,' Joss said, 'particularly on Sundays. My dad says the police ought to do something about them.'

Slowly we started to eat again and Joe expressed the indignation we all felt when he said, 'If we find out who they were we'll kill them!'

'Who?' Andy asked. 'Who'll kill them?'

'Us,' Joe said. 'You and me and Blaster and Joss and the rest. We stick together.'

Joss nodded. 'We'd better. Fagso's mad with us. He'll bash anybody who mentions about Blaster's dad beltin' his backside.'

'That's not all Blaster's dad did,' Joe said. He chuckled and held his finger and thumb about an inch apart. 'He made Fagso's old man look about that big. Fagso's mad about that, an' all. And he's 'specially mad with Blaster and me and Midge and Bill 'cos we were there and we saw it. He'll kill us if he ever gets us on our own, but if we stick together he won't be able to do a thing.'

'We might even stop kids having to pay him a shilling a week,' I said.

'Protection money!' Joss growled.

'Most of them's First Years,' Joe said. 'Little kids, like Specky Miller, there. Some of them like paying it. It makes them feel big. We do one thing at a time, Blaster. First we look after ourselves by sticking together. If that works we might start looking after little First-Year kids.'

'We don't know it'll work,' Andy Phillips said. 'If Fagso rushed us you don't know what'd happen. He's a killer. He reckons he can fight a dozen.'

I could see uneasiness in the eyes of all of them as they considered Fagso and destruction.

'I bet you've never seen him fight a dozen,' I said. 'He's a bully, and bullies are cowards.'

'Not Fagso,' Andy said. 'He's no coward. Last time he was in court it was for assault. He half killed a man one night in Cronton. A *man*! Put him in hospital.' He shook his head. 'Fagso's no coward.'

'I'm not sure he's a bully,' Ticker Price said. 'He's different from other bullies. The trouble with Fagso is he doesn't like anybody and he's got it in for everybody.'

'We stick together,' Joe said to reassure himself as much as the others. 'All the time we stick together. There's safety in numbers.'

We stuck together at four o'clock, marching down Holt Lane like a little army. Fagso wasn't waiting for us in the wood. Ginger Evans was there with Willy Oakes and Charlie Millman, two 3B boys who were in Fagso's gang. They were all smoking.

'Fagso getting scared?' Joss Hardy called.

Willy Oakes spat. 'Thompson kept 3R in.'

'Good thing for you lot, too,' Ginger said. 'Fagso's after you lot!'

We stopped. Bill Perks said, 'I'll be after you if you don't shut you mouth, Evans!'

Joss Hardy sneered. 'The bob-a-week kids!'

We walked on down Holt Lane to the buses. The Fagso boys kept quiet, but I could sense their fury as they watched us. Joe Belshaw was telling me about his father and how he worked on the furnaces at Robinson's in Grimthorpe, and how it was so hot there it could dry a man up.

'Turns some men into drunks,' he said. 'They drink gallons every day on the furnaces and they get so that they can't do without it. But my dad only drinks tea. Never drunk beer in his life. Doesn't hold with it. He's taking me fishing on Sunday to the reservoir up on the moors.'

'There's pike in that reservoir,' Andy Phillips said.

Joe nodded. 'My dad caught one that weighed sixteen pounds.'

'Bet he did!' Joss Hardy sneered.

Joe swung on him. 'I'm tellin' you, Hardy! I was there and I saw it. Nearly everybody in our street had a piece of it that night. There's some monster fish in that reservoir. You can come with us if you want, Blaster, on Sunday.'

I'd never fished in my life and could see little point in it unless you were starving. Yet, out of all the gang, Joe had chosen to invite me and I could not thrust such friendship aside.

'I haven't a rod and line,' I said.

Joe snorted. 'We've got bags of tackle! My dad'll fix you up. You ask your dad can you come. If he'll let you we'll pick you up about ten on Sunday.'

'What about *your* father?' I asked him. 'He may not want me.'

'It'll be O.K. Don't you worry. We always take somebody with us. Midge Burnett'll be coming if he's all right by then. Fresh air's good for him, and his dad knows he's O.K. when he's with us.' We reached the buses and Joe tapped my arm as we pushed through a swarm of boys. 'You tell your dad you'll be O.K. with us, Blaster.'

My mother and father were in the garden when I got off the bus and I felt that they'd been waiting for me. My mother's quick eyes darted over me and my father said, 'Well, son? Everything all right today?'

I nodded. 'Of course. What did you expect?'

My mother sighed and smiled. 'Nothing more than a little mayhem and arson.'

My father grinned at her and then said to me, 'Which do you want first? Tea or judo?'

'Tea,' I said.

I was hungry. That's the great thing about school

meals. They give you the appetite of an elephant.

We sat in the kitchen and ate tea-cakes and strawberry jam. I didn't eat too much because there was the rich smell of something cooking in the oven and I knew that supper was going to be good. My mother and father were talking about the dragon design she was working on.

I said, 'They've nicknamed me "Blaster",' and they grinned.

'It's true,' I said. 'Me! Blaster!'

They laughed. My mother laughed until she almost choked while my father laughed quietly as he always does. I waited for them to calm down.

'It isn't as funny as all that,' I said. 'You wouldn't think it so funny if they started calling you "Blaster".'

' 'Course I wouldn't,' my father said. 'But I didn't try to blow the hill away. You did.'

'I like it,' my mother said. 'It sounds rugged and reliable. Somebody must have a sense of humour.'

I sniffed. 'Charlie Harris! He invented it.'

'Who's he?' my father asked.

'Our Form Master. He's the one who sent me to the Headmaster. Some sense of humour!'

'You've got him wrong, son,' my father said.

My mother nodded. 'You certainly have! I had a picture of a desiccated little man who hates boys, but it's the wrong picture. Mr. Harris has a sense of humour.'

'So he's human,' my father said.

I shook my head. They didn't know Charlie Harris. Anyway they were grown-ups. Only a kid could taste the sourness that was Charlie's soul.

8 The Scent of Doom

Midge Burnett was back at school the next day. He came late and Mr. Mason kept him in his room for a long time so that it was almost Break before he found us doing Woodwork with Timber Thompson. Timber's hair, face and glasses were greyed over with wood-dust. He nodded at Midge and Midge went to the bench he shared with Andy Phillips and took out his work.

I had a good long look at him. It was the first time I had ever seen a boy who'd almost drowned. He seemed to be no different. His eyes were as gentle as a lamb's and they flitted nervously about the room. His skin had the delicate softness of a young girl's; the softness a woman tries to fake with power and cream. He was fragile and pink and afraid.

At Break we clustered round him and the questions started.

'Did you swallow gallons of water, Midge?'

'What did old Mason say?'

'Bet you didn't half scare the fish.'

'Did you go unconscious?'

'Did you think of all your past life?'

'What did old Mason want, Midge?'

I listened to all this. Midge, too, listened, now and then opening his mouth as if to say something. He kept glancing past Specky Miller and a couple of First-Year kids who were there, eyes and mouths gaping. He was mixed up and near to panic and I turned round and saw that he was looking at Nicker Edwards and Ginger Evans, standing together at the end of the bike-shed, their heads close. They were watching Midge and they were worried and suddenly I knew why they were worried and why Midge was afraid.

His eyes were big and watery, and Joe Belshaw, seeing them, bellowed, 'Clear off, the lot of you!'

The questions stopped. Among First- and Second-Year kids Joe's authority was never doubted. Most Third-Year kids, even Prefects, respected him enough not to rattle him.

'Go on!' he growled. 'Clear off!'

They went away, grumbling, like hyenas the lion drives off his kill. I stayed and Joss and Ticker and Andy and Bill Perks stayed.

Joe was still growling. 'They're worse than a bunch of girls!' He looked carefully at Midge. 'You O.K. kid?'

Midge nodded and I said, 'He's scared because it was Fagso's gang threw him into the canal. Wasn't it, Midge?'

Immediately I was sorry I had spoken. I wanted to show how clever I was and my cleverness had destroyed Midge. The pinkness faded from his face like magic and left him white and near to weeping. The others were all staring at him, but he stared at me.

'How did you find out?' he whispered. 'I never said.'

'I might have known!' Joe said through his clenched teeth. 'You told old Mason?'

'You tell the coppers, boy,' Ticker said. 'They'll put Fagso away, they will.'

Midge was shaking his head. 'I haven't told anybody and I'm not going to! They'd do me! They said they would!'

'Evans!' Bill said. 'It was *his* red knob I saw! And the big kid was Fagso! Nicker Edwards would be there and there was another. Who was it, Midge?'

'Willy Oakes,' Midge said.

'But why?' I asked. I could scarcely believe it. 'Why did they do it? Go on, Midge. Tell us. You're safe with us.'

'You won't let on you know?' Midge said.

Joe grunted. 'We'll massacre them! Tell us, kid. We'll see they don't touch you.'

'It was Fagso,' Midge said. 'Don't tell him you know about it, will you? They caught me up along the towpath. I tried to keep in front of them but I got puffed. They started pushing me about and laughing and I told them they wouldn't be doing it if your dad was there, Stew. I started to cry and I told Fagso I'd seen your dad clout him. Fagso got mad. I've never seen him like that before. He was silent mad. He went pale, like he was going to be sick, and he got hold of me and chucked me into the canal as if I didn't weigh anything at all. Then they stood on the bank shouting and laughing; except Fagso. He was still pale and he seemed to be watching me and not seeing me. I kept going under and coming up and I heard one of them say, "*He can't swim!*" They stopped laughing then. I think they were scared. They didn't know I can't swim. Then I think they saw somebody coming and they all ran away like mad.'

Midge stopped and we stood there and felt some of the terror he must have felt.

He said, 'But don't tell them, *please*. I don't want to see Fagso like that again. He scares you worse than ever when he's like that.'

'You ought to have told your dad,' Bill said. 'You can't let them get away with it. They'll throw somebody else in and next time me and Joe may not be there to get him out.'

'The coppers,' Andy said. 'Like Ticker says. You go to the coppers and they'll look after you. They'll give you protection.'

Joss grinned. 'And you won't have to pay them a bob a week.'

Midge's lip was trembling. There was panic in his eyes again. 'I daren't! Don't tell anybody, will you?'

Joe put a hand on his shoulder. 'Don't you worry, kid. They won't worry you from now on. We're going to fix them.'

The whistle blew and we drifted back to Woodwork with our minds on the destruction of Fagso's gang. Ginger Evans, the loneliest boy in the world, slouched along behind us. Joe hung back at the door to wait for him.

'We know, Evans,' Joe said quietly. 'It wasn't Midge who told us. It was Blaster who guessed. You tell your mates we know.'

Ginger sneered. 'You won't be able to do anything about it.'

'How about this?' Joe said and gave him a punch like a piston in the stomach. Ginger doubled up, groaning.

'I'm going to do that every day. Evans,' Joe said. 'I'm going to keep on doing it till you own up to old Mason.'

Timber Thompson came bustling along. He blew upwards over his face to clear the dust from his glasses and he peered at Ginger.

'Something wrong, Evans? Stomach-ache?'

'He isn't feeling so good, sir,' Joe said. 'In fact he's bad.'

'It'll be the rubbish you ate at Break, Evans,' Timber said. 'A slab of soggy toast the size of a tombstone, if I know anything about it. Look after him, Belshaw.'

I don't know how Joe looked after him but it was a long time before they came back to Woodwork. Ginger's eyes were red and the lids puffy.

Joe winked at me and when Timber had gone into the stock-room he whispered, 'I told him! He knows we're going to keep on until we've got revenge for Midge.'

All day there was the scent of doom in the air. After dinner, three Prefects — three big Third-Year boys — followed Fagso everywhere he went. Even he had some respect for the authority their badges represented. He snarled at them a couple of times, but they just grinned. Once Fagso stalked over to our gang and stopped, staring at Joe. Ginger and Nicker Edwards were behind him.

'I'll be seeing you, Belshaw,' Fagso rumbled. 'Ginger told me. I'm going to put the boot in, kid.'

It wasn't so much a threat as a statement of what was going to happen. His eyes moved slowly to Midge.

'You snitched, kid. You shouldn't have. I'll see you.'

'You'll see all of us,' Joe said. 'The whole gang.'

Fagso smiled and walked away and for a time none of us spoke. I think we were all puzzled by his quietness and I knew that the other boys were afraid. I wondered if I too was beginning to be afraid; if fear, like measles, could be caught from those already infected. This was no blustering boastful Fagso. This was a new Fagso who quietly menaced.

'I told you!' Midge whispered. 'He'll kill me now he thinks I snitched.'

'He's a nut case,' Joss said. 'He's round the bend and that's a fact.'

'How about if we tell old Mason?' Andy said. 'It couldn't do any harm.'

' 'Course it could!' Midge almost screeched. 'Fagso'd be bound to find out then he *would* kill us; me, anyway. I wish I'd never told you. There isn't one of you'd be any good against Fagso.'

Joe thoughtfully patted his shoulder. 'It's O.K. kid. We'll look after you. If we all stick together he won't be able to do a thing.' He sounded less certain of himself than before.

We wanted to get out promptly at four o'clock, but Charlie Harris didn't hear the bell and it was after four when he stopped. We rushed out, hoping that Fagso had been kept in, hoping for any way of avoiding the battle we all knew must some time be fought. And we kept together like sheep that see the wolf's teeth. We marched down Holt Lane; Joe, Midge, Joss, Bill, Ticker, Andy and I all in a tight bunch trying to draw courage from each other, but, instead, I think, giving each other fear.

Fagso was waiting for us. He was standing, legs astride, out in the middle of the lane like a gunman in a Western.

'You other kids can clear off!' he called. 'It's Belshaw I want this time! Belshaw and little snitchy Burnett!'

In an instant we were no longer together. Midge turned and scampered back and Andy chased after him. Bill and Joe stopped, waiting, in front of Ticker and Joss. I kept on walking towards Fagso, excited and glad to find that I was not afraid.

Fagso saw Joe and went for him in a lumbering sort of rush which took him past me. I don't think he even saw me. I think that he had only Joe in his eyes and he went past me like a gorilla. Without a thought I stuck out a foot and Fagso flew over it and landed on his face. He hit the road hard, slid along it and lay for a moment or two grunting and spitting.

Slowly he turned himself on to his hands and knees and looked at me. There was a graze on his forehead and a bleeding cut on the back of his hand. He hated me with his eyes, crouching there in the road and gathering himself for another rush. I watched him and I thought about myself. My feet were springily planted and my arms were held away from my body, hands open, ready. My heart was thumping quickly, but it was excitement, not fear, that was tingling through my veins.

Then two legs, slacks neatly clipped round ankles, appeared behind Fagso and there was Mr. Harris, his bicycle left behind with Bill Perks. Fagso and I had spent some seconds in a little personal world in which there had been no place for Mr. Harris or anybody else.

'I've always wanted to see some boy put you on your face, Brown,' Mr. Harris said.

Fagso sprang to his feet and spun round.

'You're a bully, Brown,' Mr. Harris went on, 'but this time I'm not going to do anything about it because you were getting the worst of it, for the first time in your violent life.'

'He tripped me!' Fagso grumbled. 'He couldn't ha' done if it he hadn't tripped me.'

'Don't argue with me, boy,' Mr. Harris said. 'You were getting the worst of it and I think you'd have gone on getting the worst of it. Now go home and take those nasty friends of yours with you.'

Fagso swung round and when he faced me he was smiling with his lips while his eyes hated me. Shoulders thrust forward, he went down the lane.

'You, Evans!' Mr. Harris called. 'And Oakes! Come out of that wood and go home!'

Ginger Evans and Willy Oakes came shamefacedly out of the trees and set off after Fagso.

Mr. Harris was looking at me and smiling a little dried-up smile. 'You must be trouble-prone, Stewart. You spend your time up to your neck in it. However, this is the first time since coming to Cronton you've done something I approve of.'

'Yes, sir!' I said, and his smile became a real one.

He took his bike from Bill Perks and rode after

Fagso and the two 'bob-a-week' kids.

I told my father and mother about it. I said, 'You were right. Charlie Harris is human, after all. He does his best to hide it, but he's human.'

Then I told them about Joe and Midge and Fagso.

'Joe?' my father said. 'He's the big boy who looks like a bloodhound, isn't he? And Midge is the little boy who was walled-up in the cave.'

He looked at me in that casually searching way of his. 'Think you can handle it, son?'

My mother put her cup down with a crash. 'You mean can he handle the Brown boy — that juvenile gorilla?'

He nodded and she went on, 'But should we expect him to handle a boy like that? Jimmy isn't used to them. In fact he isn't used to *boys*!'

'But he has to learn,' my father said.

She sniffed. 'He needs some help. You should go and have a word with the Headmaster.'

'Who are you talking about?' I asked her.

She wrinkled her forehead. She's a very pretty woman, my mother, even though she's getting old, and she's prettiest when she's puzzled.

'I'm talking about *you*, Jimmy. Who else?'

'I was wondering,' I said. 'If you're talking about me I ought to be given a chance to join in, shouldn't I? So I don't want John to go to see old Mason.'

'*Mister* Mason!' she said.

'It might not be a good thing,' my father said. 'The Headmaster can't be expected to protect Jimmy twenty-four hours a day. It might be better if I went to see young Fagso and his father. I could scare the pants off them.'

'You can't be expected to protect me, either,' I said. 'I've got to look after myself sometime so I might as well start now. Trouble is I don't know if I can.'

'It doesn't matter,' my father said. 'What matters is that you'll have tried.'

I shook my head. 'I don't know. He's a big kid, is Fagso.'

'Your judo's coming on fine. You're pretty good.'

'Fagso put a grown man into hospital. He was in court for it. A grown man!'

'I found him easy enough,' my father said, 'and I didn't use judo. I used brute force.' He stood up. 'Let's go and practise, son.'

The cut-grass patch was by now so dead you might have wondered if grass had ever grown there. It was a tiny desert island in an ocean of rolling vegetation. I did my breakfalls first, while my father watched, and then for half an hour he rushed me and struck at me and I threw him. To me it was a wonder how easily I could throw him with my hands gripping his pullover and my right foot thrust into his stomach as I rolled backwards. It seemed that I used his energy to make him weightless. We kept on until I was tired and then we practised ground defence. We were still at it when my mother came from the house with Mr. Ferriby. He always looked clean and trim. He had an easy grace of movement like a cat's.

He gave my father an odd look. 'I hope Jimmy isn't thinking of trying this on me.'

My father chuckled as he dusted himself off. 'Judo's a defence. If Jimmy's attacked he'll use it.

I'm trying to get him to the stage at which he'll use it without thinking about it.'

It was Mr. Ferriby's turn to chuckle. 'If this catches on they'll have to include it in teacher-training. Otherwise the next schoolmaster who forgets himself and clips a boy across the ear may find himself flying through the window. Very bad for morale.'

'Danger-money,' my father said. 'That's what they'll have to pay you.'

'They should be paid it now,' my mother said. 'Anybody who has to train dangerous animals like the Brown boy deserves danger-money.'

Mr. Ferriby scowled as if displeased but was too polite to voice displeasure. All he said was, 'You mean Fagso? He's not so bad, you know. I sometimes wonder how much of it's his fault.'

My mother sniffed. She knew where the fault lay.

Mr. Ferriby dragged her thoughts away from Fagso.

'Speaking of animals,' he said. 'I've had a phone call from Professor Paynter. It looks as if Jimmy's dinosaur is a new species all right. The Professor's in touch with people in the States. If it is new it'll be named after Jimmy.'

'Then it ought to wear a kilt,' my father said. 'Stewart tartan.'

They strolled laughing back to the house and I went to the quarry. I didn't want to be pally with Mr. Ferriby. I liked him in the classroom, but I still blamed him for robbing me of my dragon. Anyway, it isn't a good thing to be pally with teachers; not if you want to be pally with kids, and I did. There were so many boys I liked at Cronton that not even Fagso and the bob-a-week kids could spoil the pleasure I was finding in companionship.

I stayed in the quarry for some time. It was so quiet in there that I could forget there was a world outside. I left it only after night, creeping across the country, found the quarry and filled it first with darkness. When I got back to the house supper was ready and Mr. Ferriby had left.

'He couldn't stay,' my father said. 'Fiona asked him.'

I said nothing. If I'd said I was sorry it would have been a lie but a polite one, and if you aren't supposed to tell lies I don't see that politeness makes them any better.

During supper my father said, 'We were talking about Fagso. Interesting boy.'

I waited and he went on, 'Seems he gives trouble to some of the teachers. One or two of them can't control him at all.'

'Of course they can't,' my mother said. 'The police are the only people who are trained to deal with hooligans.'

My father swallowed and shook his head. 'Wrong, Fiona. Some of the teachers have no trouble with him at all.'

'They'll be the big tough young men,' she said. 'They're the only ones who are fit enough to deal with him. He's a bully so he'll be afraid of anybody who can hurt him.'

'Wrong again,' my father said. 'Mr. Thompson and Mr. Dodge, Jimmy. They never have any trouble with Fagso. What are they like? A couple of heavy-weight boxers?'

I snorted. 'Timber's an old bloke . . .'

'Listen to him!' my mother groaned. 'After little more than a week!'

I let her finish and then I went on, 'And Dauber Dodge! He's weird! He has a beard a foot long and he only ever speaks in whispers. Fagso's bigger than him, a good deal bigger. He teaches Art.'

'And Timber?' my father asked. 'Woodwork?'

I nodded and he said, 'That's it! Fagso likes Art and Woodwork and has some talent for each, it seems. It isn't the teacher: it's what he teaches.'

'A teacher worth his salt,' my mother said, 'can interest children in any subject.'

'Nonsense,' my father said. 'Boys like Fagso are interested in the subject and a good teacher will develop their interest. Fagso's an anti. He's very nearly anti-everything, but he's particularly anti-authority. It's his home. He could be reclaimed, like the clay I reclaim, and if it isn't done soon he'll go to the dogs completely. But with his home there isn't much chance. Father — a drunken lout; mother — a virago; sister . . . well, we won't talk about the sister.'

That reached an uneasy corner of my mind from which troubled thoughts had recently been coming.

'Why haven't I got a sister?' I asked. 'Why didn't you ever get a sister for me?'

They forgot about Fagso. They looked at me and then at each other.

'We never got around to it, son,' my father said.

'There's been so much to do,' my mother said.

'John's career as a potter; mine as a designer.'

'What about my career as a brother?' I said. 'Even Fagso's got a sister. Joe Belshaw, Bill Perks, they both have sisters. Some kids in our Form have got brothers *and* sisters!'

They just looked at me, uneasily or guiltily, I thought.

'You never talked this way before you went to school,' my father said. 'You were happy enough when you were by yourself. You weren't discontented then.'

My mother stood up, her eyes very bright. 'Reading, writing and arithmetic aren't the only things boys learn at school.'

9 The Broken Pot

There was no trouble at school next day. There was just a morning mystery. Midge Burnett was absent again and Joe spent the time until Break looking as puzzled as a hen that's lost its chickens. He kept sighing and shaking his head. Pop Hawkins thought Joe was having trouble with logarithms, but I knew that Joe was heavy with the sort of responsibility only a kid can have.

At Break he told us about it.

'I called for him this morning! His mam told me he'd gone to school! Well, he isn't here. Can you beat it? *Midge!*'

'I don't believe it,' Joss Hardy said. 'Midge playin' wag!'

'He wouldn't have the nerve!' Andy Phillips said.

Joe sent a glare at all of us. 'Well where is he, then? Eh? You tell me!'

None of us could tell him.

'I bet he comes after dinner,' Bill said. 'You know what he's like. He'll have been taken bad and gone home.'

Joe growled. 'His mam was off out all day. That's why Midge had gone early. She was just going when I got there. She was going shopping in Grimthorpe and she told me she wouldn't be back till this afternoon.'

'But *Midge*!' Bill said, shaking his head. 'He'd be too scared. He wouldn't know any place to hide.'

I knew why Midge, driven by a fear greater than his fear of authority, was playing truant, and I knew where he would be hiding.

'The quarry!' I said. 'He'll be in the cave!'

'He's scared of it,' Joss said.

'He's more scared of Fagso,' I said.

Joe nodded. 'You could be right, Blaster. After dinner I'm going to look for him.'

As soon as first sitting was over he borrowed a bike from a 2B boy and set off for Farley. He was away for more than half an hour and we waited for him all the time at the school gate, the whole gang of us in a fidgety, nervous group, talking about Midge and keeping our eyes open for Fagso, set on destruction. But Fagso was smoking at the back of the bike-shed where, Joss told me, the Prefects never went.

'They know if they go they'll find Fagso smokin',' he said, 'and if they find him they've got to report him. Then somebody'll get beaten up.'

'You mean the Prefects are afraid of him?' I asked.

Joss gave a twisted grin. 'What do you think?'

Then we spotted Joe wobbling up Holt Lane with somebody, like a sack, on his crossbar.

'It's Midge!' Andy Phillips said, screwing up his eyes.

'There's trouble for Joe,' Ticker Price said. 'Riding two on a bike's trouble if a Prefect sees you, boy.'

But no Prefect saw Joe. He cycled wearily up the slope and stopped, falling sideways on to one foot. Midge disentangled himself and rubbed his backside where the crossbar had pressed a numbed groove into it. Joe's face was red and stern. He nodded to me.

'You were dead right, Blaster. He was in the cave. All I could see of him when I got there was two white eyes in the darkness, like a cat at night.'

'Why'd you do it, boy?' Ticker asked.

Midge blushed and shook his head.

'Scared,' Joe said. 'Like Blaster said he was scared of Fagso. He thought I must be Fagso when I got there. Never thought anybody else could be lookin' for him. I told him we'd look after him.'

'Who's going to look after us?' Joss asked, with a nervous grin.

Ticker patted Midge's head. 'You want to tell your dad, boy. You tell him to go to the police.'

'No!' Midge said, desperately shaking his head. 'I keep telling you! Fagso'd get me! He wouldn't care how long he waited. He'd still get me.'

'He's right,' Bill Perks said. 'Fagso's like that. He never forgets.'

Joe growled through clenched teeth, 'What we could do with is a kid who could belt Fagso. That's all we need. If one kid belted Fagso we'd never have any more trouble from him.'

'You're the biggest,' Joss said.

Joe nodded. 'He'd murder me. When I'm bigger I'll have a go, but right now he'd murder me.'

'And Charlie'll murder Midge for not having a sick-note,' Andy said.

'Somebody'll have to write one for him,' Joe said. He looked at me. 'You, Blaster. You're a good speller and you talk more like a grown-up than a kid.'

So I wrote Midge's note, inventing a headache for him and forging his father's signature, and at registration Mr. Harris read the note while we watched his lips silently moving and his eyes scanning the lines. When he'd finished he said, 'Feeling better now, Burnett?'

Midge said, 'Yes, sir,' and Mr. Harris nodded.

I felt no shame at the success of my deception. Instead, because it was Charlie Harris I had deceived, I felt triumphant. Joe rubbed his hands together under his desk and winked at me.

There was no trouble at four o'clock because nobody was waiting for us in the shadows under the trees. We felt our hearts lift and we hurried down Holt Lane to the buses, passing between fields of brilliant green where young wheat speared up out of the soil.

It was the same on Thursday and Friday. It seemed that for some reason Fagso was late leaving school each afternoon, and without Fagso his gang kept out of our way. Fagso was their courage as well as their strength and they feared that our collective anger would drive us to avenge Midge's half-drowning in the canal.

On Friday when we reached the bus Joe went to the driver who was leaning against the radiator, out of the cool wind, smoking a cigarette. The rest of us climbed slowly into the bus.

Bill Perks blew out his held breath and said to me, ' 'Nother week over, Blaster. Soon be Whit.'

'Soon be Monday,' Joss Hardy said. He prodded Midge's chest. 'You keep in over the week-end, young Midge. Then Fagso can't get you. You too, Blaster. Fagso'll do you for tripping him up. He'll kick your teeth in if he gets you.'

I wasn't afraid of meeting Fagso. I felt nervous and excited when I thought of it, so that my stomach began to ache, but I didn't feel Midge's paralysing fear or the panic fear of Andy Phillips.

'I'm going fishing on Sunday with Joe and his father,' I said.

'So am I,' Midge said.

Joss nodded. 'You'll be O.K. with Joe's dad.'

'You can come fishing in the morning, if you want, Blaster,' Joe said. He was climbing into the bus. 'You meet me at the canal, by the bridge to the old station, about ten and I'll show you how to fish. Midge's coming, aren't you, Midge? And our kid'll be there. What about it, Bill? You coming?'

Joss grinned. 'How about your Molly, Bill? Is she coming?'

Joe glared and stalked down the bus towards him and Joss giggled and scuttled away from him and stopped and said, 'Hey! Look who's here!'

Everybody turned round and there was Ginger Evans's red head rising slowly, like another sun, from behind the last seat where he had been hiding from us.

'Evans!' Joe said. 'One of the bob-a-week kids!'

'Let's do him!' Bill said.

The driver was fitting himself into the seat behind the wheel. I could see his eyes in the mirror, watching us.

'Settle down you lads!' he called. 'Unless you'd rather walk it home.'

So Ginger was saved for another day of revenge and Joe came and sat beside me and talked about fishing.

There was no judo practice for me after tea because a load of clay had arrived during the afternoon and my father wanted to put some of it through the pugmill. This was his first load of the rich-red local clay and he was quietly excited about using it. I stayed in the house after tea and did the week-end's homework.

It was evening and there was only a red smudge over the hills to show where the sun had been when I took my head out into the cool air to clear it. My mother was cleaning palettes in the studio and from one of the outbuildings there was coming the slow grinding of the pugmill. I went across to the door and looked inside for my father, but he wasn't there. The pugmill was slowly extruding its long sausage of clay and the room was chilly dark.

I walked round to the front of the old barn, where the lane runs alongside it, and there, leaning on our gate, was Nicker Edwards, leering at me as if he thought I should be pleased to see him. I wasn't pleased. I went up to him, scowling, and he just leered and leaned more heavily on the gate and I knew he must be getting borrowed courage from somebody.

'You can clear off!' I growled at him.

His eyebrows went up. 'Charming! Is that any way to talk to a mate?'

'We don't want your sort round here,' I said.

'I'm waitin' for Fagso, kid,' he told me, as if that gave him the right to be there.

'We don't want his sort, either.'

'You tell '*im* that, kid.'

'I will, when he comes.'

Nicker's leer turned into a grin and I saw his smoke-browned teeth. 'When he comes! He's here! Been here ages!' He nodded. 'He's in there with your old man.'

He was nodding at the open door of the throwing-room. I swung away from him and, with his titter following me, I went to the door. The light was on. My father was bending over one of the potter's wheels and close to him was Fagso, watching my father's hands draw up a vase out of a dollop of spinning clay. I saw the clay on the wheel and my father's fingers working their magic on it: I saw his head and Fagso's, together, with the electric light making haloes round both of them: I saw Fagso's face shining in the light, and shining too with interest and wonder. There was no vestige of his old brutishness, so absorbed he was.

My father kept dipping his fingers into the water. 'It's not so difficult,' he said. 'Not once you've found the knack. Get your clay centred on the wheel and the rest isn't so difficult. You can have a go in a moment.'

'Bet I'll make a mess of it!' Fagso said.

My father nodded. ' 'Course you will. I did the first time I tried. You've got to make a lot of messes before you can turn out something worth looking at.'

'What's *he* doing *here*?' I said, my voice so tight it almost cracked.

They both turned and my father's mouth opened, but I didn't let him speak. I pointed at Fagso and rushed straight on.

'You know who *he* is? He's the bully who threw Midge into the canal! He's the bully who scares the little kids into paying him a shilling a week!' I could hear my voice echo round the room as if it were somebody else's coming to me from a distance. There was a roaring of angry blood in my ears and the electric light had turned dull red. 'He's the hooligan who smokes and swears! He put a man in hospital! He's been to court . . .'

Fagso glanced at my father and suddenly heaved himself past him and across the room and out through the doorway. I listened to his feet thudding away down the lane and the roaring blood steadied in my veins and the redness died out of the light. I was trembling. My squall of rage had gone and taken my strength with it.

My father stared for a time at the doorway as if he thought Fagso might come back. He stared at the wheel still spinning beside him and suddenly he crashed his hand down on the half-formed vase and in a second turned it back into a lump of clay. He switched off the wheel and watched it while it turned steadily more slowly until at last it stopped with the clay dollop in the middle of it.

Still watching it he said, 'What you just did was as bad as anything Fagso ever did. Why did you do it? Why, son?'

I knew that his anger had come after mine and that he had waited for it to die away before he spoke.

'But . . .' I said. 'You know what Fagso Brown's like!'

'I know what he's supposed to be like. I know what you say he's like and what everybody else says. I was trying to find out for myself.'

'Don't you believe about him throwing Midge into the canal?' I asked.

He nodded. 'Of course I do! I was trying to find why he threw the lad in.'

'Because he's a bully and a hooligan. That's why! You hit him yourself the other day. You put him over your knee and you gave him a hiding.'

'Because he was smashing the fossil,' he said. 'He was being a vandal and I treated him as vandals ought to be treated. But he wasn't a vandal just. He may have come here to smash something, but he didn't. He was just a kid with fingers itching to get at the wheel.'

My father walked slowly out of the throwing-room and I followed him. The evening was quickly turning into night and a blackbird was emptying its heart of song in one of the old fruit trees. We stopped at the end of the barn and looked across at the hills and my father put his hand on my shoulder.

'He was interested in the wheel, Jimmy — really interested. I was going to show him how to throw a pot.'

'You've never even shown me.'

'You've never asked me, son. You've sometimes watched me working at the wheel, but you've never been unduly interested. Now Fagso, he was more than interested. He was hypnotized. I thought when I found him in the throwing-room . . .'

'You *found* him?'

He nodded. 'I'd just started the pugmill and I thought I heard a noise at the front of the barn. I went round and there was Fagso looking at one of the wheels and slowly turning it with his hand. I remembered that he's good at Woodwork and Art. He's good with his hands. So I asked him if he'd like to see how it worked. He was cautious at first — cagey; wouldn't come near me; like a kicked dog not trusting me. Then when I got the clay on the wheel and started to draw it up he forgot he was scared. He came and watched and he talked to me. For five minutes he wasn't a bully or a vandal or a hooligan: he was a youngster who'd found something he wanted to do; something worth while. And I was going to let him do it. That's the way to turn the Fagsos of this world into decent citizens.' He paused and I felt his fingers bite into my shoulder. 'If I could have that lad for long enough I'd turn him into a man.'

We started to walk towards the house. The lights were on and my mother was whistling in the kitchen.

'And then I came,' I said.

'And then you came, Jimmy, and you spoiled it. Do you understand what you did?'

I think I understood. I think I understood why he'd been so angry, although I couldn't see why Fagso should matter to him.

'It was the same as if I'd broken a pot you'd just made,' I said.

He nodded, hard. 'Right, son! I think I might have done something with the lump of clay you call

Fagso. I still might if I ever get the chance again. But now you'll have to try it your way. Fagso's going to be angry and resentful. He'll be dangerous. He'll want to get even with you. Try to remember your judo. If you can throw the lump of clay about I might still make it into something useful.'

He never said a word to my mother about it. They were both like that. They never told each other things about me: they never snitched.

She looked up when we went in blinking into the light of the kitchen.

'Supper's ready, you men,' she said.

When we were sitting down my father nodded at me and said to her, 'He's going fishing in the morning. Any objections?'

'Not if he brings back a salmon,' she said.

I grinned. 'Out of the canal! Have you seen it? Anyway, I'm only going to watch Joe Belshaw. It'll be different on Sunday. I'll be fishing then.'

She looked, puzzled and pretty, at my father. 'Did we know about this?'

'I did. Forgot to mention it, Fiona. Joe Belshaw's the boy who looks like a bloodhound. His father's coming round on Sunday morning to collect Jimmy and they're going on to the moors where there's a reservoir full of pike.'

'Pike are big,' she said. 'You've never even caught a tadpole, Jimmy.'

'I can learn,' I said.

My father chewed thoughtfully for a time and then he said, 'You're learning an awful lot just lately, aren't you, son? And I don't mean only at school.'

10 The Fight

I went fishing the next morning. It was one of those mornings that happen only when you're a kid. It was bright and the air was full of the scents of earth and water, of trees and plants and blossom. There were more birds than I had ever seen.

I walked towards Cronton and took the lane down to the old railway. It was a narrow lane almost smothered under hawthorn running wild. I climbed out of it and on to a humpback bridge and looked over the wall. The canal cut a shining swathe through the countryside for half a mile and then curved away towards the moors and lost itself behind Cronton. Along the towpath I could see a fishing-rod poking out over the water and, behind it, Joe sitting on a basket with Gladys beside him. I slid down the steep little slope to the towpath.

The surface of the canal had a steely shine and smoothness broken occasionally by the bursting of a gas bubble or by the nose of an exploring fish. I'd been on the towpath only for a few seconds when Gladys saw me and ran to meet me, calling, 'Sh!'

'I'm not making a noise,' I told her as soon as she reached me.

'Joe keeps getting a bite,' she whispered, walking along beside me and trying to match my strides.

Her face was pink and glowing with such friendliness that I don't think she could ever have made an enemy.

'Has he caught anything?' I asked.

She shook her head and giggled. 'He never does in the canal. My dad says there aren't any fish in it. He says our Joe only takes worms for a swim.'

'I'm using bread, clever!' Joe grumbled. His hand was on the butt of his rod. He gave me a quick nod and turned back to the float which angled up out of the water and bobbed weakly from time to time. I knew nothing about fishing, but I knew that the rings expanding from Joe's float meant that somewhere down in the dark water a fish was tasting the bait and I caught some of Joe's excitement. I stared at that float, willing it to dive, but instead the ring stopped growing out of it and it became quite still.

Joe lifted his rod and drew in the line.

'Pinched my flippin' bait!' he said. 'Little tiddlers they'll be, sucking it off. They want to go and bring their dads. Feel like having a try, Blaster?'

He started to squeeze bread on to the hook and Gladys said, 'Here's Molly and Bill!'

Joe glanced along the towpath, He was blushing. 'That's the end of fishin',' he said. 'What's she want to bring that transistor for?'

They came towards us, walking in noise, the noise of strum and beat and scream.

'Molly Perks!' Gladys accused. 'You've got lipstick on!'

Molly shrugged her shoulders and Bill grinned.

'She won't have by the time we get home,' he said. 'My dad'll kill her if he sees her with it on.'

'He's a square!' Molly flashed. 'My mam says it's O.K.'

'Caught any, Joe?' Bill asked.

Joe shook his head and Gladys said, 'He was getting a bite. It pinched his bread. Come on, Molly. Let's go to the bridge and listen to some pop.'

'Hear about Fagso last night?' Bill asked.

I glanced at him. 'Fagso? What about him?'

'Seems he was in a fight outside the *Crown and Cushion*. Two big kids — about eighteen they were — were standing on the corner talking and Fagso comes up with Nicker Edwards and he starts a fight. Nicker says Fagso'd about half killed both of them when some men came out of the pub and stopped it. Nicker says he never saw Fagso so mad; reckons the two big kids never did a thing. They were just in Fagso's way.'

'How do you know about it?' Joe asked him.

'Saw Nicker when I was on my way here. He told me. He was going for Fagso.'

'You didn't tell him where you were going?' Joe said.

Bill shook his head. 'Not me, mate. But our Molly did. Girls are daft.'

Joe groaned. 'P'raps we'd best clear off.'

'Why?' I asked.

Joe glanced along the towpath, where Molly and Gladys were sauntering away from us, taking the transistor's tinny noise with them. 'There'll be trouble if Fagso comes. We haven't got all our gang. There's only three of us.'

'Four!' Bill said, grinning. 'Here's Midge. The mighty atom!'

Midge was running towards us. He darted between Molly and Gladys and came panting up to us.

'You wanna watch it, kid!' Joe growled at him. 'You aren't supposed to run like that.'

'Fagso!' Midge wheezed. 'He's coming! Got Nicker and Ginger with him!'

Joe grabbed his basket. 'That's it! We're off!'

'I'm not,' I said. 'We've as much right to be here as anybody else. I came to watch you fish.'

'Well you aren't going to,' Joe said, ' 'cos I won't be fishing. Use your head, Blaster! We can't fight Fagso. There aren't enough of us. It'd be like trying to fight a buffalo. He'll soon be here.'

'He's here now!' Bill said.

Fagso was lumbering down the slope to the towpath. Behind him were Nicker and Ginger. Gladys turned and scampered back to us, but Molly waited. We could only see her back, but I could imagine her eyes, part-hidden by the glossy hair which hung like half-drawn curtains down each side of her face, sleepily watching Fagso. He was a boy, a dangerous, exciting boy. She fancied herself as Beauty before the Beast.

To Fagso she was an empty kid and with one sweeping arm he knocked her out of his way. Bill Perks growled. Fagso was near enough now for me to see that I was the one he was looking at.

'You other kids beat it!' he said. 'It's Stewart I want!'

Joe swallowed, but he stayed beside me. Gladys

shouted, 'You're a coward, Fagso Brown! I'll tell the police!'

Midge trembled, 'Let's run!'

I said, 'I'm not running!'

I walked to meet Fagso and stopped a couple of yards in front of him. My feet were apart and I was on my toes.

'What do you want?' I asked him.

'You!' he said.

He didn't stop and he didn't hurry. He just kept on like a tank and when he was close enough he swung his right fist at my face. My head was so clear, my brain so sharp, that I saw everything as if it were in slow motion. I saw the fist coming and I knew what to do. I caught Fagso's wrist in both hands, I spun round and bent forward, at the same time jerking Fagso's arm down. He flew over me and landed on his back in front of me. He was easier to throw than my father was. He was smaller and much lighter and he had no skill in judo, and no idea that I had any. He hit the towpath with a crash that knocked the breath out of him and I laughed when I thought of the time I had spent practising breakfalls. In a flash I saw the faces of the others; Joe's and Bill's comic with wonder; Gladys's shining with worship; Nicker's and Ginger's unbelieving.

In my triumph I tried to be clever. I stood astride Fagso and got a straight armlock on him and he bit the back of my leg so viciously that I yelled and jumped away. There were tears in my eyes and through them I saw him scramble to his feet.

This time he came at me more cautiously, crouching as he came. I had been cool before: now I was cold and confident and I knew what he was going to do. As soon as his right foot lashed up at me I turned my side to him and lifted my right foot so that Fagso's leg jarred into it. I felt his shin grate along the heel of my shoe and I heard the whistle of his indrawn breath when the pain scorched him. But the force of the kick staggered me, and so furious was his animal courage that even the fire in his leg could not stop him. He swung his fist at me again and I ducked, but not quickly enough. It seemed that a club hit me over the ear: that my head exploded in a burst of light. I fell sideways and yet, while falling, my body was taking over from my numbed brain and doing the things that long practice with my father had trained it to do. I fell and rolled and saw Fagso's boot sweep past me. I rolled again and I was on my feet before Fagso controlled his swinging kick and turned to face me.

I could hear a high piping voice screaming and I knew Gladys was hurling her kid's fury at Fagso. My head was clearing and I was ready for him. He looked a mess. He was scratched and torn and panting. Too many cigarettes were poor preparation for this long fight. He crouched in front of me, watching, waiting, worried and angry. He was baffled and uncertain what I would do. I put my hand up and stroked my swollen ear.

Instantly he leapt at me, reaching out to clutch me, and almost gladly I took a quick step inside his arms, grabbed his leather jacket in both hands, put my right foot in his stomach and rolled backwards with his rush. As soon as my curved back hit the ground I thrust my right leg out straight and catapulted him over me. Against the sky I saw Fagso flying, arms and legs in a tangle, and I heard the splash as he went into the canal and I felt the water rain down over me.

Slowly I turned on to my hands and knees. I was panting and there was bedlam all about me. Joe, Bill and Gladys were dancing and cheering like mad: Molly was trying to look like a rescued maiden: Midge was frightened: Nicker and Ginger were tearing away so quickly that they must have felt certain that they would be tossed after Fagso. They were afraid. They had seen Fagso, the unbeatable, beaten by a smaller boy and they could not understand. In one instant Fagso's tyranny had ended and he was no longer big enough for them to shelter behind.

Suddenly the shouting stopped and I heard Bill's voice in the silence.

'He can't swim!'

Still on my hands and knees I looked again at Fagso, out in the middle of the canal. His arms were lashing in the air and his face, eyes and mouth wide open, was just below the surface. I saw the water flow into his mouth when he tried to shout and all I heard from him was a drowned gurgle.

Then Joe Belshaw was going through the water like a torpedo. I didn't see him dive into the canal but there he was, planing across the surface. As Fagso sank Joe reached him and drew him up into the air and tried to turn him on to his back. But Fagso struggled. Panic had got him and he grabbed Joe.

'He'll drown our Joe!' Gladys wailed.

But Joe knew how to deal with desperate Fagso. He pushed Fagso's head under and held it there so long that I began to be afraid.

'You'll drown him!' I heard myself shouting. 'You'll drown him, you fool!'

But Joe didn't drown him. He lifted Fagso's head above the surface again and Fagso was quiet, his head lolling on his shoulder. Joe turned him on to his back and ferried him to the bank right in front of me. I looked down on Joe, blowing the water off the end of his nose, and Fagso, with his long hair in wet points clinging like an octopus to his white face.

'Catch 'old of 'im!' Joe gasped at me.

I grabbed Fagso by one shoulder and Bill took the other and together we couldn't haul him up the bank. Gladys took him by the collar and gave a girlish tug. Molly turned her transistor up and said, 'If you don't get him out of that canal he'll be dead.'

Then Joe was beside us, pushing Gladys out of the way, and the three of us hauled Fagso on to the grass at the edge of the canal.

'On his face!' Joe said.

We turned Fagso over so that his head hung down the bank and the water ran out of him.

'Right!' Joe said. 'On his back again!'

Fagso's face was still white and dead.

'I'll give him the kiss of life,' Bill said.

'You won't,' Joe said. 'You don't know how to do it. I'll do it. You hold his head up.'

Then Fagso gave a sort of bark and his eyes blinked open. He looked up at the three of us and took a deep breath.

'You O.K., Fagso?' Joe asked.

Fagso grunted and sat up. He shook his head, looked up at me and shook his head again. Then he pushed Joe out of the way and climbed slowly to his feet and his boots squelched. He shook himself like a dog and walked along the towpath away from us without a word. His wet jeans were clinging to his legs and he kept combing his hair back with a quick movement of his hand. We watched him go towards Cronton. Somehow he seemed to be smaller. He was a small solitary boy with nowhere to go. He was loneliness in wet jeans and jerkin and I was sorry for him.

There was neither sorrow nor pity in Bill's voice when he said, 'That was smashin'! I bet you've put a stop to Fagso, Blaster.'

Gladys shook her head like an old witch. 'Poor Fagso!' she said. 'He gets good hidings at home and now he's had one outside.' She turned to Joe. 'You'd best run home, our Joe. Next thing, you'll have pneumonia.'

Joe was beginning to shiver.

Molly, her big eyes fondling me, said, 'My, but you're tough, Jimmy! You just threw Fagso all over the place. You aren't half strong. I bet you could beat anybody.'

She made me feel sick. She could switch on artificial emotions as readily as she switched on her transistor.

I grabbed Joe's arm. 'Come on! Gladys is right. You ought to get home.'

We all went tearing along the towpath and into the lane and where it joined the main road we saw our old car just drawing up and my father sticking his head out of the window.

'What happened, Joe?' he said. 'Did you fall in or were you pushed?'

'He dived in,' I said.

'For Fagso!' Midge panted. 'He life-saved Fagso, Mr. Stewart!'

'And you'll never guess how Fagso got in the canal!' Gladys said.

'You tell me,' my father said.

'It was your Jimmy!' Molly said. 'He threw Fagso in! Just like he was a sack of potatoes!'

My father looked at me. 'It happened, then?'

I nodded. 'And the judo worked fine.'

For some reason he didn't look very pleased. 'Jump in,' he said. 'All of you. It'll be a squeeze, but you can manage. We'll take Joe home.'

It was a squeeze all right, and nobody wanted to be squeezed against wet Joe, although he tried to get as close to Molly as he could.

She said, 'Don't you touch me, Joe Belshaw! You're all wet!'

I glared at her and said, 'He isn't the only one,' and Gladys smiled at me.

The old car wheezed a bit at first, but slowly it picked up speed and when he was satisfied with the engine noise my father said, 'Now tell me about Fagso.'

I started to tell him, but the others kept butting in and taking the best parts from me. Sometimes there were three of us talking at once. We were almost in Cronton by the time the tale was told and we waited for my father to say something.

He said, 'Tell me how to get to your house, Joe.'

'You turn left here, Mr. Stewart,' Gladys said. She was in the back, on Molly's knee. 'Then you turn right and that's our street.'

'I'll see you tomorrow, Blaster,' Joe said. 'We'll be round for you about ten. Then it's school again on Monday. I'm sort of lookin' forward to school. There won't be any more trouble from Fagso.'

Bill, also in the back, and nursing Midge, said, 'No more bob-a-week kids.'

'I hope not,' Midge whispered.

'Don't you worry, kid,' Joe said to him. 'Any trouble from Fagso and we'll set Blaster on him.'

'You will not!' I said. 'He'd kill me next time.'

My father nodded at me and grinned. 'We'll call round to see him,' he said. 'We'll go as soon as we've seen Joe home. Who knows where Fagso lives?'

They all knew. We dropped Gladys and Joe off at their house, but Bill and Molly and Midge stayed with us in the car all the way across Cronton to the forgotten street where Fagso lived in a house squeezed in the middle of a row. All the houses were the same, but most of them had polished doors and scrubbed steps and window-sills scoured clean with stone. But not Fagso's. Fagso's house looked as lonely and defeated as Fagso had looked when he walked away from us on the towpath.

My father got out of the car and said, 'Come on, Jimmy. The rest of you stay where you are.'

He rapped on the door's cracked paint and we waited for a time. Bill Perks's nose was flattened on the window of our car and behind him Midge was crouching; a frightened Midge still afraid of Fagso and vengeance. My father knocked on the door again and this time it was wrenched open by a fat woman with a cigarette in her mouth and a nicotine stain on her lip and her hair in tight curlers.

'Who're you?' she said. 'We don't want any.'

'My name's Stewart,' my father said. 'Your boy and mine had some trouble, Mrs. Brown.'

Her eyes went as blank as a fish's and she was pushed aside and Fagso's father stood in the doorway. He looked at my father and all his truculence vanished.

'It's you . . from Farley,' he said. 'Some trouble? Raymond just came in. He fell in the canal.'

My father nodded. 'I know. I wanted to be sure he's all right.'

Mrs. Brown, back somewhere in the dinginess of the house, snorted. 'All right! He's never all right!'

'I'd like to have a word with him,' my father said.

Mr. Brown nodded doubtfully. 'I reckon you'd best come in, then. Our house ain't much, but you can come in. He's upstairs putting some dry clothes on.'

I'd never seen a house like that one. There was neither light nor colour in it and even the air was stale. I saw a table strewn with unwashed pots, an easy chair with broken springs and a carpet so thin my feet could feel the boards underneath it. I don't know what they called the room but they ate in it, they watched television in it and the stairs went up from one corner of it. Mrs. Brown was in the kitchen at the back. I could hear her muttering to herself.

'Raymond!' Mr. Brown bellowed. 'You come down here, my lad!'

He glanced at my father. 'You said more trouble, Mr. Stewart?'

'Nothing to bother about,' my father said, 'so long as your boy's all right.'

Mr. Brown sniggered. 'You can't kill our Raymond. Once or twice I've tried it myself.'

'Tried what, Mr. Brown?'

'Tried killin' him, that's what!'

My father was looking straight at Mr. Brown and I scarcely recognized him. At home we never saw his face so granite hard. He said, 'I thought you were his father.'

Mr. Brown snorted. ' 'Course I'm his father! What do you think you're talkin' about?'

'I think I'm talking about the way a father treats his son,' my father said. 'What do you think I'm talking about?'

Mr. Brown flushed and swung towards the stairs. 'Where's that perishin' lad?'

'I'm 'ere!' Fagso growled, lumbering down the stairs. 'What's up? What do you want?'

He saw us, standing in the squalor of his home, and shame chased astonishment off his face.

'Jimmy tells me you tripped and fell into the canal, Fagso,' my father said. 'We called to make sure you're all right.'

Fagso glanced at me and he was puzzled.

His father said, 'How come you fell in? And how'd you get out? You can't swim.'

'He might have drowned himself,' Mrs. Brown

shrieked from the kitchen. 'And him nearly ready to start work!'

'They were larking about,' my father said, 'and your boy tripped, Mr. Brown. That right, Jimmy?'

I nodded. I always knew that my father was good: now I knew him to be great. 'That's right,' I said. 'He tripped over me.'

'You wanna be careful,' Mr. Brown said to me. 'You might have drownded him.'

'You know what boys are,' my father said.

Mr. Brown sniffed. 'I ought to. Trouble, that's what they are. Look at our Raymond there. He's only interested in trouble.'

'You're wrong,' my father said. 'He's interested in pottery. He came round to Farley last night and gave me a hand.'

Mr. Brown glared at Fagso. 'You never told us.'

'You never asked me,' Fagso growled at him.

'When are you coming again, Fagso?' my father said. 'I want to show you how to throw a pot; you know, on the wheel. Jimmy wants to learn too.'

Fagso looked at me. 'Mean to say you can't do it?'

I shook my head. 'I've never tried, but I can learn.'

'So can I,' he said.

My father nodded. 'That's it, then. You come round in the morning. Jimmy's going fishing, but you and I can have a bash.' He turned to Mr. Brown. 'Would that be all right?'

Mr. Brown was looking at Fagso as if he'd never seen him before. 'It'll be all right, I suppose.'

Mrs. Brown, arms folded fatly across her chest was at the kitchen door.

'If our Raymond's helpin' you, mister,' she said, 'how much are you goin' to pay him?'

'Shurrup, Mam!' Fagso grumbled.

My father might have been looking at a cockroach. He wasn't. He was looking at Mrs. Brown.

'You've got it the wrong way round,' he said. 'He isn't helping me. I'm helping him. I'm going to give him the chance to do something useful; something he may have some talent for. I'm going to teach him how to create beautiful things with his hands. In other words, I'm taking an interest in him and it's a pity you've never done the same.'

He turned his back on her belligerence and said to Fagso, 'In the morning, then. And don't be late.'

'What time, mister?' Fagso asked.

'Ten o'clock,' my father said. 'And don't bring any cigarettes with you. There's no smoking.'

He made for the door, leaving Fagso with a glow in his eyes, and I followed him. The others, all ears and eyes, were waiting for us, but they took one look at my father and didn't say a word. We dropped them in Cronton and we were almost back in Farley before my father's anger had died. He chuckled suddenly and began to sing one of those lilting Scottish songs he sings only when he's done something very special.

'You sound as if you've just made the best pot ever,' I said.

He nodded. 'I think I may have, son.'

When we turned in at our gate we saw Mr. Ferriby and my mother standing outside the drying-room. She was holding a tall, unglazed vase.

'I've just been showing off our new mark,' she said to my father.

Mr. Ferriby took his pipe out of his mouth. 'The dragon of Farley!'

My mother was looking at me in that way mothers have — so that you feel they know the answer before they ask the question. Yet they always ask it. She did.

'And what have you been doing?'

'Watching Joe Belshaw fish,' I said, and told her the truth without telling her all of it.

'Did he have any luck?' Mr. Ferriby asked.

My father was grinning. 'He pulled out a monster.'

To turn my mother's attention on to something else I took the vase from her. Impressed in the bottom of it was my dragon. My mother had not robbed him of his old ferocity. It was all there, concentrated in his tiny shape.

'It's good, Fiona,' I said.

'It's *Ornithomimus stewarti*,' Mr. Ferriby said. 'I heard from the Professor this morning. They've named it after you, Jimmy.'

My mother, determined and pretty, was still watching me. 'Fishing isn't all you've done,' she said.

'He's been teaching Fagso a new skill,' my father said.

She glanced at him. 'Judo?'

I nodded. 'It worked like magic.'

'Skill's often mistaken for magic,' my father said. 'Tomorrow I'm going to start teaching Fagso another skill so that he can work his bit of magic.'

He took Mr. Ferriby and my mother, a hand on the arm of each, towards the house, and they left me standing in the sunshine. It's brightness was making the grass glitter. I wandered through the old garden to the quarry and I looked at the cave and the blast-marks on the rock and at the place where my dragon had been. Somehow I didn't miss it any longer. The quarry was so peaceful that there was no room in it for ferocity.